Learn to Say No if You don't Want to Say Yes

Renu Saran

DIAMOND BOOKS

ISBN : 978-81-288-3423-3

Publisher : **Diamond Pocket Books (P) Ltd.**
X-30, Okhla Industrial Area, Phase-II
New Delhi-110020
Phone : 011-40712200
E-mail : sales@dpb.in
Website : www.diamondbook.in

Learn to Say No if You Don't Want to Say Yes
By - *Renu Saran*

Contents

Why This Book?

If you find it difficult to say 'No,' most of your time would be spent in doing such tasks that you would not be keen to do. If this status quo continues for a long time, the feelings of petulance and despondency naturally keep on increasing in the mind of the person in question. Due to this, the relationships with kin and friends can become sour. If you do not say 'No,' you would start feeling that you have control neither over your time nor your life.

When you hesitate to say 'No,' a situation is created in which you feel that water is spreading around you and you are unable to close the tap. When you want to say 'No' to the request of a person but say 'Yes,' the feeling of grief and anger swells within you. Not only that, the level of stress also rises inside you. Thus, your health can be adversely affected due to these two causative factors. The first reaction (of your body) can be in the poem of headache. Saying 'No' means closing the tap that's already open. It also means stopping the flow of external pressure. That way, the right to take decision remains in your hand. Further, you also retain your control over your time and life. If you say 'No' directly and openly, your self-confidence is also reflected that way.

Those people, who hesitate to say 'No,' have many types of notion in their mind. They believe that good, decent people consider it their duty to do the tasks of others. They over that if someone says 'No,' it means that he or she is deemed to be selfish and having rough manners. They go on to state that if people hear 'No,' they are hurt, insulted, or they might become angry. Thus, they fear that people would not like them (if refusal is the answer). If you to have all these notions cropping up in your mind, change them quickly, else your life can become miserable.

Often, due to the mistakes or illusions at the thought level, a person hesitates to say 'No.' This is the first illusion which means – you feel as if you are insulting and showing contempt for the other person. The second illusion is – you feel that the other person may not find it easy to digest your 'No.' The reality is that if 'No' is uttered properly and honestly, people accept it happily. Sometimes, the relationships of people become deeply cordial only due to this refusal. Since, you say 'No' with honesty, the other person also expresses his feelings with clan and asks for help, without any hesitation, in the future as well.

It is difficult to say 'No' for the first ever time. If you practice regularly, you acquire this habit. You need to adopt different techniques to say 'No' under different circumstances. In this book, complete information sets have been given about the intricacies of the art of saying 'No'. Many fine methods have been appended in this book which can be adopted by any person to become an expert in the art of saying 'No.' That way, he would be able to make his life prosperous.

●

1

Welfare: Boon or Curse?

When we find that there are scathing attacks from the people while we try to communicate them, or when we observe that violence rules the roost while we try to put across our point to others, it is good to note that some good people are still present in our society. Don't we need an atmosphere full of decency and elation around us? Under such a condition, what can be the meaning behind giving a sermon of doing less welfare (for others)?

The major reason behind the rising levels of aggression is that we believe too much in welfare. Whenever we are hurt to the core, or whenever someone misbehaves with us and moves ahead, we allow others to use us. Alternatively, we do away with our peace of mind and comforts in front of others. Thus, we appear to be much more suave in the viewpoint of others. Thus, we appear to be much more suave in the viewpoint of others. The more we accept the pressure excited on us (by others), we are prepared to do anything to avoid the head-on conflict and maintain peace. And the more we avoid this situation of conflict, the more we increase the quantities of displeasure and dissatisfaction within our own selves. Later, these quantities (of these feelings) become explosive within us!

When we are unable to express our thoughts and emotional experiences, we alone suffer. We lack the capacity to present our inner world before the outer one. Due to this very reason, our welfare becomes a bank for us instead of becoming a boon for us.

We all know that every person's conduct is decided

according to the environment he or she lives in. People are taught that if they do the tasks of all, a good image is formed in the mind of all. If you do good, you get good. We must always help others. Such types of good thought are not at all bad. We are also not giving you the sermon that you should not become noble, caring and gentle.

Read some episodes that have been appended ahead. You would find that many of them are familiar.

Neera was sitting on a sofa. She had a cup of tea in her hand. She had just sat on the sofa. The telephone bell rang.

"Hello Neera, I am Ruchi. I know that you are free now, given that your children have gone to school—and you husband is in office. You are alone at home. Hence, a fabulous idea has flashed across my brain. A sale of Jewelry is going on in the city. You come in your car. I shall accompany you. In fact, I wanted to take my car to come to you but it's old. I think it would be better to go by your car. You reach here in half an hour. Is that OK?"

"Listen Ruchi, I am not doing anything as of now. But I wanted to read something. Moreover, some household chores were waiting...."

"Oho! Leave old things. If you stay at home, you would continue to be stifled. If you move out of home, you would feel fresh. You can read at any point of time. I don't want to listen to anything. You are coming!"

Thus, an unwilling, hesitant Neera was forced to go to the Jewelry store to attend to her friend's demands. Why did she not say 'No' directly and bluntly? It is not a difficult word. But for Neera, saying 'No' was even more difficult than conquering Mount Everest.

Now, let us study the following episode. "Ritesh! That's good I met you before we left office. Someone has to stay here, for an important fax message is to be received. I think you should stay."

"But Sir, it's my wife's birthday today. I must reach home a bit early." "Why are you talking like a henpecked husband? What's more important for you—your career or your wife's birthday?"

"She would be very sad. I cannot disappoint her."

"What are talking, Ritesh? You were never like this. I have always considered you to be a young man who is always dedicated towards his work. I have been thinking about giving you a promotion."

"All right sir, I shall call up my wife and tell her that I am staying here. I would also tell her that I would be late today." "That's like a good boy. I know that you are a capable man."

When Ritesh goes home, he would have to face his wife—a woman in a rage.

Now, read the following episode:

"The soup is very cold. I think I should tell someone to heat it up."

"There are so many people in this party. Only you are having some problem with this soup?"

"But papa..."

"You should learn some manners. What would people think?"

"This is ice-cold..."

"Stop it, for my sake."

"Alright."

That girl would have to drink cold soup; her suppressed anger would also be imbibed by her along with the soup.

Now, read the following episode:

"Zeenat, you are looking gorgeous."

"Oh uncle, I have worn the suit gifted by you."

"Please come and melt in my arms!"

"But uncle, I am your (maternal) niece."

"You are young and beautiful. Youth is granted to humans only once in their lifetime."

"But...."

"No one would ever learn about this, Zeenat. Come, don't waste time."

"OK, uncle...."

That way, an illicit relationship would commence.

Now, read the following episode.

"Leena, come to my room after this meeting."

"But sir, I am supposed to go to my room and take rest after the meeting."

"Why have I brought you here, on the official tour of the company?"

"Sir, don't take me wrong. I am not a girl of loose character."

"Do you want the job or not?"

"OK sir, I shall come."

That way, a helpless girl is forced to spend nights with her boss.

Now, read this episode.

"Sweety, I am Seema on this side."

"Seema, are you coming for dinner?"

"Listen Sweety, I have called up in this connection only. My mother has become sick all of a sudden, so I won't be able to attend the dinner. I am sorry but you know very well..."

"Oh! It's OK. I have prepared fully well. But you are also helpless."

"I hope you won't mind...."

"No, no! It's OK. I won't mind."

"Good! I shall call you up later. Bye!"

A peeved Sweety would switch off the phone and curse her own self for preparing so much food. Now, read the following episode.

"Raju, have a puff!"

"No! I don't smoke."

"What are you talking? Don't you want to become a man?"

"No! I don't like cigarette smoke."

"All newcomers in this hostel say so. Taste it just once."

"The warden may see me...."

"He is asleep. Take a puff...."

Thus, an intelligent boy takes a first step on the road to drug addiction.

There are many such episodes which tell us that a person sacrifices so many things to remain a good human being, he also causes harm to his our self while he does so.

When the feelings, stifled inside the mind of such persons, explode, they hurt their own selves. Then, they go back to their shell and become gentleman. They pretend as if everything were normal!

Such people believe in remaining gentle and innocuous due to their nature. They believe in giving to others. So, when others demand something from them, they come to their knees and give the thing being demanded from them. They do not know how to oppose for the sake of protection of their interests. They do not want to tell others that they are bothered to the hilt when they are forced to do a piece of work. They do not want to tell others how much bothered they are when they have to do work that way. They are always fearful—they think that if they say so, the feelings of others may be hurt. Thus, they think, other people may become angry with them. They think that if they oppose their friends, they might lose them. They think that if they say 'No', the family may witness increased bitterness. They are fearful that all people would be angry with them and that the situation would go out of control. Such noble people are always bothered by the ghost of the fear of result. Hence, their role becomes limited in life. Being gentle becomes a bane for such type of good people. Those, who are noble and gentle to the core, are always afraid of saying 'No'. They always nurture the notion that if they say 'No', something terribly wrong may happen, or they think that something offensive to others or beyond the human boundaries may transpire (if they refuse to do something or accept a piece of advice). So, they hesitate to say 'No.' The reality is that a person can convert even his good nature into an art, and that person also learns to say 'No' according to his own will.

When a person learns how to change his behavior, he gets better control over circumstances. He learns to take decisions by becoming free from the force of emotions. Uncontrolled emotions make a person helpless and weak. For this purpose, it is not necessary for you to entirely change your personality. Examine and test all the alternatives available to you. Analyze all alternatives. Then, change your behavior.

Noble people are very decent, wise, compassionate and liberal. They know how much important it is to help others. That's why they consider it to be very important to behave with every person in a sympathetic manner. They welcome people with enthusiasm. They never hesitate to do the tasks of others. If a person becomes less noble or less helpful, it does not mean that he should do away with those qualities with the help of which this world can be made a better place. Becoming less noble means that the person should also pay attention to his own welfare; this act is very important in the present era.

2

Initial Formulae

The initial formula is like a (testing) touchstone due to which your inner vision and awareness would increase. Thus, you would learn what kinds of loss you would incur if you become a gentle and noble person beyond a certain limit. You would observe that this problem is so complex that it is very difficult for you to identify those elements that and make you handicapped or helpless. On the other hand, being noble and gentle may also not be a big problem for you. However, some complications can arise, we can ignore them completely.

Some from among you people may feel that it is very complex problem. But it is not that complex. There are some facets of your behavior that are conducive to your interests. You also know this fact very well.

In this book, a basis has been provided to understand that problem easily. Thus, you have got an opportunity to examine your own behavior with ease:

(A) The ways through which you present yourself as gentle.

(B) The primary sources of your absorbing behaviour.

(C) The emotional experiences that have made you limited and secluded.

We shall throw light on all aspects of your behavior. You may be aware about them up to a level but may be finding it difficult to comprehend them.

For this purpose, we would motivate you to do the maximum practice that is possible. We would suggest that you jot down all emotional experiences, thoughts and comments in a diary after reading the exercises and questions appended in the chapters that follow.

In this book, an effort has been made to give a new speed to your thoughts so that you may become aware of the new thinking about becoming too gentle or noble (towards others).

As a human being, you learn how to behave on the basis of your environment. If an effort is made with awareness, the learnt behaviors can be modified. You go through various chapters of this book. As you do so, you would be able to give sharpness to your thoughts and beliefs. Thus, you would be able to use your virtue (of being noble) as a boon, not as a bane.

●

3

Are You a Noble Person beyond the Need?

What Would You Do?

You have obtained a ticket to attend the concert of a famous singer. But your mother-in-law's birthday falls today, so there is a party to be attended to congratulate her.Pick one option:

(A) You would attend the birthday party. You would not mention the music concert. However, you would remain peeved.

(B) You would make a false excuse over telephone and tell your mother-in-law that you are required to work late in office.

(C) You would tell your mother-in-law without any qualms that the music concert of your favourite singer is being organized. You would also tell her that you have decided to attend that concert. You would add that you would love to have dinner in her company the very next-day.

What Would You Do?

Your neighbour is going out of town for one week. He requests you to take care of his pet dog. Although you are not irritated by the dog, you certainly are irritated by the idea of cleaning it and looking after its needs. Pick one option:

(A)You would say that it's not a matter to worry about. You would take the dog home and spread (old) newspapers on the entire floor of your home.

(B) You would say that there is problem in taking the dog under your control. But you would add that mechanics are likely to come to your house and take up some repair jobs. In such a condition, the dog would not be looked after with finesse.

(C) You would tell the truth that you may find it troublesome to take care of the dog and clean it properly. Thus, you can add that you would not be able to keep the dog for one week.

What Would You Do?

You are in your bedroom, with your newly married wife. You are about to have sexual intercourse with her. So, you have started doing some foreplay acts, viz., kissing, hugging, caressing etc. You expect your wife to do something to you so that you become highly eager to do coitus with her. Pick one option:

(A) You would lie down and leave it to her will.

(B) You yourself would do such an act, hoping that your wife would repeat the same act.

(C) You would tell her about the act on your own.

What Would You Do?

You are a computer expert. You had done the task of your colleague (on computer), it was her personal task. Now that colleague comes to you time and again to get her task done. Thus, your task suffers. Thus, you are supposed to stay after office hours to complete your task. Pick one option:

(A) You would smile upon seeing her. You would tell her that there is no problem in extending a helping hand to her. You would add that you would stay for extra two hours to complete your pending work.

(B) You would say to her that the computer has developed a fault and that you would not be able to do her piece of work, given that you have not been able to complete many pending tasks.

(C) You would clearly tell her that you had helped her once but you would not be able to do so time and again.

In all of aforementioned situations, our dilemma would be—which method is to be adopted? If you know that you are much gentler than the limit requires you to be, you would probably like to choose the first or second solution available to you. You would be unpicking and wearing to do so. You can also imagine that had you been strong and courageous, you would certainly have liked to pick the third alternative. But that too is also not good.

There is no fixed right or wrong method in the case of behaviour. There is no formula or directive that you may depend upon under all circumstances. No solution arrives from the sky.

In the chapters that follow, you would get information about how you can become an expert in bringing about changes related to behaviour. As a person who can absorb (knowledge and concepts), you would be nurturing many expectations about how you would like to lead your life. You can be critic of your own self as well. It would happen when you find that you are not getting success in changing your behaviour and way of talking with others. In such a situation, you start feeling that you have failed!

That objective of this book is not to consolidate such thinking as may increase the number of fiascos. The behaviour that is correct is straight. The behaviour that is wrong is zigzag and weak.

This book would not show you the right path. Rather, it would show you another path along with many alternatives. You would always have the right to choose the procedure for a particular situation.

The term 'noble' or 'gentle' is being deliberately used here. It defines a behaviour under which people go away from their true personality, ambitions and goals.

But it is not necessary that a behaviour, which is inspired by 'welfare,' may necessarily be wrong. This issue has been discussed in this book. We have mentioned in it how you can use your behaviour, inspired by the spirit of welfare to serve your own interests.

It is not incorrect to be good and noble. This can be an ideal method of dealing with others. Since such persons are sensitive, thoughtful, compassionate, wise and empathetic about the needs of others, being noble for the sake of achieving mutual coordination, consent and felicity can prove to be a useful virtue.

But when you are noble beyond a limit—you become thoughtful beyond a limit—you give consent to every thought. In that case, problems start cropping up. When you are unable to decide what type of behaviour you should adopt and you can remain noble by behaving in a different manner, then problems start raising their ugly heads. In such a situation, this word becomes a symbol of weakness, despondency, languor and restlessness.

When it is necessary to become decent, ethically self-restricted and humble, the 'noble' or 'gentle' behavior is appropriate. But when you are being deceived, or when you are being exploited, or when you are being misused by others, or when you are being dealt with opprobrium, or when you are directly being misguided, in all these situations, it is better to be courageous and conspicuous. But if you think that other people would not like this, or if you think that they would feel insulted, or if you can visualize that they would they would become angry with you, and that's why you do not think about your interests, in such situations, your 'noble' or 'gentle' behaviour certainly becomes a curse for you.

Those, who are excessively noble, believe that they do not have any second alternative. They think, "I am like that only. I cannot change myself." They remain very much troubled. That's because they neither adopt alternative methods to escape these troubles nor do they think of adopting such methods.

Sometimes, we do such tasks as we should not do. We ought to follow some rules because we are social beings. We have to live in different groups—family, home, work place, neighbourhood, city, state, country etc. Nevertheless, same occasions arrive on which we eschew our own desires and needs by keeping the broad interests of our society in full view.

This means that if you agree to say back in office (after office hours) and help your boss in giving replies to letters (and so, miss an opportunity to take hot tea at home, dutifully served by your wife). It means that you collect donation for the people affected by deluge, even if you may not like the idea of 'begging' for money by moving hither and thither in a procession (along with the residents of your locality).

You can go along with your wife to the market to purchase curtains for your home. You can leave your favourite TV programme for this purpose. You can go to meet your sick relative and ask him how he is recovering. You can meet him instead of taking rest at home. You can take a leave of one-half day from your office and use that time to attend the Parents-Teacher Meeting (PTM) of your son. You can do away with your exercise routine in a morning; in that time, you can help your friend resolve his typical problem (of married life).

These tasks are not very difficult and you would feel that you are supposed to do some other tasks instead of the priority or previously planned tasks. But you would have the solace of doing minor types of sacrifice for the sake of broader interests. So, that way, you are succeeding in increasing the depth and sensitivity of your relationships with your family, friends and society. When you do these tasks, you are naturally peeved but this feeling of peevishness is removed.

When you see that others are quite ecstatic (due to your contributions). Thus, you feel that you have contributed, from scratch, towards your account of good deeds. That way, your self-confidence becomes stronger.

But when rules take the place of exceptions in your daily life due to the aforementioned types of sacrifice, the balance starts getting disturbed. Then, you start feeling that due to these genres of 'sacrifice,' your personal life has started taking a drubbing and it is staggering. That way, your account balance becomes zero in your bank of good deeds. On the contrary, the feelings of anger and pain as well as desperation start being credited in that account. Thus, your self-confidence level starts receding very quickly.

Besides, if you are excessively noble, people also do not like you. They think that you are weak. They find that you are in a state of indecisiveness. They observe that your morale has gone down and that your thoughts are unclear. Thus, they do not want to leave any opportunity of bothering you. You say, "Whatever you say is right." Or, you say, "I don't have any objection." Upon hearing this, some people would be peeved to the core because they do not expect such types of passive response from others.

How Much 'Noble' Are You?

You must define whether your behaviour is a bone or bane for you. Put yourself in the broad context of "noble behaviour" and decide where you stand. A list has been given ahead which is concerned with the behaviour that assimilates and absorbs. Read it carefully. That way, you would be able to identify yourself in those fields in which it becomes difficult for you to take decisions. You would also be able to identify those fields in which you feel balanced and are able to control your decisions.

This is an opportunity for you to self-analyze—till what limit, would there be the need to change your natural behaviour. You can identify some emotional experiences which you face when you unwillingly try to change your behaviour.

We would not like to state forcefully that the behavioural patterns included in the list (appended ahead) fall in the right or wrong category. When you would decide that a particular behaviour is harmful to you, it can be included in the category 'wrong.' For example, for some people, avoiding conflict at any cost can be a very correct option and thus, they do not have to face any trouble at any point of time. On the other hand, for some other people, warding off (circumventing) conflict means that they would never be able to put their dissent or disagreement put on record. Thus, they think that they would never be able to talk about their own interests—later, they would feel heavy within due to the fact that they could not say 'No!'

We quickly comment on our tasks. We say this is good and that is bad. If you identify a thing as a problem (at your personal level), that is a problem for you. It's just possible that it is not a problem for some other person. Hence, it would be incorrect to declare that all types of 'noble' behaviour are not correct.

This book would help you decide what your difficulties are and what you can do to remove them. But that does not mean that you should start implementing new rules to lead your life in a correct manner.

Some questions related to self-analysis have been

appended ahead. Write numbers against each question. Use the following table to give responses to the questions.

Grading System

Never	1
Sometimes	2
Often	3
Always	4

Do you do the following?

- Even if you have not made any mistake, you ask for pardon.
- You ask for permission, even if there is no need to do so. For example, you say, "May I get you a cup of tea?"
- You defer or avoid conflict at any cost.
- Whenever something goes wrong, you consider yourself to be guilty.
- You worry—what other people would think (you may not know those people).
- You do not like a task. So you tell a lie to defer or postpone it. Then, you hide the lie. Then, you remain under the fear that your lie might be caught.
- You want that all people should like you, even if you do not like all.
- You find it impossible to say 'No'
- You feel that you should do everything to please others.
- You expect that others should be liberal, just like you.
- You give what people demand from you.
- You ask for forgiveness due to the bad behaviour of another person.

- When you ask for something from someone, you feel heavy within.
- When you tell a bad news, or when you listen to it, you smile.
- When people are agonized, you think that you are accountable for making them happy.
- When you tell what's in your heart, you hesitate a lot.
- You imagine what other people are thinking.
- You expect that people would take you wrongly, i.e., they would misunderstand your acts and thoughts (instead of taking them rightly).
- When others are fighting, you try to reach a settlement (between or among others).
- You believe that people are not been to listen to you.

  You avoid being a centre of attraction because you fear that others may not consider you to be an ostentatious person.
- When someone raises a question on your behaviour, you try to justify your behavior.
- You accept an attack in a silent manner. You do not show your feelings in front of others to express how much deeply others are hurting you.
- If the rules that you delineate are not followed, you expect to interfere.
- You are peeved if a kin calls you up over telephone; and you are also hesitant while talking to him.
- You take decisions on the basis of what other people expect from you.
- You try to avoid those circumstances that you cannot deal with.
- When your near and dear ones do such a thing which,

in your view, can be objected to others, you ask for forgiveness.

- You ask weak questions. For example, you ask, "Can I ask one question?" Or, you make ask, "Would it be appropriate if...."
- You are not able to tell people about your emotional experiences in a correct manner.
- When someone criticizes in a general manner, you consider it to be a personal critique (on your own self).
- You agree to do those things that are expected from you.
- You agree with others because you feel that others want only 'Yes' from you.
- When you fly into a rage, you boil from inside but at the overt level, you keep on smiling.
- You are unable to tell your life partner about your sexual needs in a clear-cut manner.
- You become angry over trifles but do not discuss big issues.
- You consider it wrong to say something to a person for your own benefit.
- You go to spend holidays at a place that you don't like but other people do.
- You give loan to people but are hesitant to take your money back.
- You have many friends, so misuse them.
- You feel that changing a decision would not be the right thing.
- You get tones of advice and the starting sentence is, "The best method for you to do this is...."
- You are unable to tell your close friend that he is

bothering you.

- When someone tells you, "I want to say something to you," you become eager to listen to him or her.
- You have to go out with someone, even if you don't want to do so, and that's because you do not have an appropriate alibi to say 'No.'
- You feel that you must remember the birthday of every person.
- When you ask something from others, or when you take something from others, you feel deep regret,
- You become angry over even not-so-vital issues.
- You do the work (at home) which is supposed to be done by others.
- When you do not return a thing borrowed from someone, you are bothered because you have not returned it.
- When you are not ready from your heart, you still agree.
- You are bothered by your promises.
- You like to select the path of least resistance because you want to avoid conflict.
- You feel that you are not better.
- You do not make efforts for your promotion.
- If you reach a place late, you express too much of regret.
- You imagine, while driving, that the driver of the vehicle behind yours is paying attention to you.
- When you give advice, you find it necessary to confirm it. For example, you ask, "Would that be fine for you?"
- When people give you gifts, you say, "What was the need of giving this gift?"

- You are told to work late in the night, or you do the tasks allocated to others.
- In any meeting, it is difficult for you to start the discussion and give a preliminary speech.
- You have to listen to praise (for you) from your colleagues and boss rarely. However, you have to face their critique in most cases.
- When someone tells you to do something, you, "Whatever you say would be right for me."
- You are not able to accept encomium (heaped on you) with decorum.
- People exploit you.
- Instead demanding a pay raise, you consider it correct to wait.
- You accept a lower price (than the right and appropriate one) in lieu of the services provided by you.
- You find it difficult to change your daily routines.
- You feel that you must attend every such party in which you have been invited.
- You take the food that you don't like, fearing that others would mind if you refuse to take it.
- If someone is making a noise, you do not consider it right to say anything to him.
- You pay extra attention on the preparation of any discussion or meeting.
- You are hesitant to buy anything or to return anything that was bought by you.
- You feel that in a social gathering or congregation, people consider you to be a boring person.
- You feel that you should not spend holiday in the lap of comfort and luxury.

- You give your phone number even to those people who you would not like to meet again.
- People tell you that are sensitive beyond limits.
- Before others ask you, you start discussing your weakness.
- You feel guilty because you are not able to pay more attention to your parents.

Checking Your Answers

Just Passing

If most of the questions answered by you get the grade 1 or 2 (i.e., never or sometimes) you are capable of deciding about the appropriate behavior in any situation. Many times, you do such tasks as you would not like to do, or you become prepared to change your behaviour, in mental terms, on such occasions but do not want to act that way. However, your normal life routines probably continue as per your wish.

You are not swept away by the thought that people would dislike you. That's because you know it is impossible to satisfy all people. Thus, in order to please others, you do not find it necessary to change your behavior. You have balanced thinking which means that your internal world is in tune with you external one. You do not change your thoughts and deeds till the extent that may bother you.

This book would help you improve those inconvenient facets of life that you would like to control more rigorously. It would help you get a new edge for your thinking.

Border Line

If most of your answers are 2 or 3 (sometimes or often), it means that some aspects of your life are not fine and you may also feel that circumstances are being controlled by someone else, not you. The spirit of welfare is not governing you; rather, it has become a reason for your troubles. You would consider it important to rectify and repair such facets from the beginning so that your behaviour may be inclined according to your interests.

You can also feel that life is full of paradox. At one point of time, you don't find any problem in keeping busy in your own self. Whatever you want, you get. You move ahead in any situation (and feeling comfortable while doing so). Then, a time can come when you are in a state indecisiveness or you are angry because you cannot reveal your emotional experiences and thus you feel very much helpless.

You know the fact that in many cases, you are successful in making the outcome of a situation conducive to your needs and goals. In some other cases, you feel so much without strength that nothing is in your hands (that you could change). Due to this paradox, your entanglement increases.

This book would help you resolve those paradoxes and thus, it would be possible for you to have balanced situation in your life. Due to it, you would be able to coordinate in a better way. Besides, the need to depend upon the charity of others would also reduce. In your brain, the picture of an ideal life is already present. This book would play a helpful role in realizing that picture.

Sign of Chaos

If most of your answers are 3 or 4 (often or always), you can understand how much serious things can be for you.

You know that you always feel that you are bowed down and defeated most of the times. You want to say 'No' but your month utters, "Yes." You are reluctant to give agony to any person's heart. You keep on bringing changes in your own self according to the wishes of others. Probably, you believe in keeping people satisfied since you are fearful that if you do not do so, you would have to face a mountain of troubles. You play the game of life according to the rules defined by you. Not only this, you also believe in the fact that such rules are controlled by other people.

Most of the times, you remain unstable, uncertain, worried, dejected, troubled and doubtful. You think that you should not remain in this condition, for it is a pathetic condition (and that you must come out of it). You do not have the feeling of attachment towards your own self and you imagine that people are taking pity on you. In reality, this thinking of yours is not wrong.

This book can help you remove the feelings of remorse due to your fate. It would tell you that you are not the only person who can be swayed away in the currents of emotions. It would help you keep strict and strong control over the difficult situations that you want to use to bring about change. Your case is not a case of complete hopelessness. There are many people who think on these lines. You do not have to remain ignored for a long period.

What Were Your Emotional Experiences?

The evaluation of your behaviour is Just the first step. It can help you identify your problem. In this Journey, there are many other important facets, beside, your behaviour.

In this book, those emotional experiences have been examined which arise when you want to do something but are forced to do something else. While reading this book, you would be able to identify your impulses and modify them according to your needs.

But we can initially check out what types of emotions were created in your mind. Did you feel a special type of process? Did you adopt a flexible posture while dealing with family, friends and people at work place? Which field is the one in which you to face the maximum number of difficulties?

Was there something in some questions due to which you were surprised? Probably, in some areas, you are not as 'noble' or 'gentle' as you probably think. And in some areas, you are much gentler than you opine to be. If someone else reads this list of yours, what would you feel?

When you were adding the marks your answers, what did you feel? Did you find it difficult? Did you have shame of any kind? Did you feel that other people can also face the problem, just like you? Did you hesitate? Did you feel peeved? Was your concentration broken?

Did you say, "I know all this but there is no need to know more"? Did you say, "I have not done anything like this before and now, I want to do it time and again."?

Did you tell your own self, "This is all rubbish and from next time onwards, I would make myself much stronger."? Or, did you think, while heaving a sign of relief, that you are getting help?

It is easy to agree in this era. Many people do not like to do anything by going off the traditional track. They think that doing this means they are trying to be selfish. The term 'selfish' is a word that is often used to rectify the behaviour of people and it proves to be effective. This is a common notion that being selfish is a bad thing and that being unselfish is a good thing.

The poor noble person does not get an opportunity to feel. What the feeling of becoming selfish really is. He also does not know how one feels when one gives priority to one's own needs for the sake of change.

You Make Your Realm on Your Own

Every time you change your behaviour, or when you think that there is no alternative available to you, you limit your expression. You can remain normal only if you do not remain consistently vigilant about what is the impact of your tasks on others.

It's not wrong to create a realm for your own. If you do not do so, you may have to live in a chaotic society. Then, the real meaning of the word 'selfish' would be—being self-centred and working for our own benefit. Then, we would see a large number of irresponsible people around us. But if the impulses that run your life are attached to the fear of insecurity, shame, contempt and criticism, the chain of behavioural patterns available with you would become very narrow. If fear always dominates you, you would remain dominated and that way, your self-confidence would continue to become weak.

Just think—what types of thought had come to your mind when you had tried to do something beyond your general, normal behavioural pattern. Then, your mind may be having a monologue as follows:

"Probably, I won't be able to do this."

"They would not like it."

"This would certainly insult him."

"He would really become angry."

When such types of thought may have cropped up in your mind, you must have controlled the desire of doing the act you really wanted to do. Let us take an example.

- "If I tell my mother that it would be very difficult for you to call her up every night, she would be very sad and I cannot afford to displease her."
- "If I tell my beloved that she looks more beautiful in long hair, she would never talk to me."
- "If I tell my boss that I have not been able to prepare my last month's report, he would think that I am incapable and thus, he would never give me any important task."
- "If I eat up the last piece of sweetmeat, lying in a plate, all people present there would consider me to be greedy and hungry."

- "If I tell him that the movie that I Had watched in his company, he would think that I do not have the sense and manners to watch TV and so, he would no longer have any relationship with me."

In all these "If I..." situations, two points are seemingly vital. The first one is—the fear of result stops us from speaking something openly or doing something overtly. The second one is—we always think more about the negative or harmful aspects of any situation or problem.

We rarely think as follows: "If I tell my boss that I have not been able to prepare the report for the previous month, he would probably order someone to help me."

"If I tell my boss that I have not been able to prepare my report, he would understand the problem and give a solution."

We create a shell or realm around ourselves which is very small in most cases. There are many rules and regulations in this realm.

If You Are More Than Noble, Then You Ought to Be for Your Own Sake, Why?"

Loneliness and Your Behaviour

When most people are alone, their true behaviour comes to the fore. They know, at that time, that no one is watching them or forming any opinion about them. So, they do not try to change their behaviour. They sing while bathing. They put their feet on the table while watching the cricket match on TV. The lick their fingers while eating. They litter their clothes in the room. They do silly acts like these.

But in such a scenario, if someone enters with a bang, these people naturally change their behaviour. Some changes are logical and useful. For example, it is considered bad to put one's finger in one's nose in full public view. But when you are alone, you do so. Only a few people do this in the presence of other people. This is called Social Behaviour, such routines or acts are not wrong either. Under this, your personal freedom is not hurt and the status quo is also maintained.

But if you change your behaviour due to the fear that people would laugh at you or consider you to be in the wrong, it would mean that you are trying to follow the rules made by you. These are the rules which are not followed by others. They were not taken into confidence while framing these rules.

We are appending one example here.

Rani, a 26-year-old girl, works for a call centre. She lives alone in a rented flat. She is a lively and jovial young woman. She likes to spoil her face in front of the mirror. She loves to dance to the tunes of songs she loves. She listens to songs at a high pitch most of the times. She performs new experiments in cooking. Sometimes, she does not know whether the food she is cooking would be edible or not. She has a pet cat whose name is Mini. She can talk to Mini for long periods (since Rani thinks that Mini understands her every word). When Rani sits down to eat, she makes Mini sit on the table, in front of her. Rani loves to wear jeans and T-shirt. Her favourite toy is teddy bear; it always remains on her bed. Rani loves environment and that's why she has put up a poster of the earth on a wall.

Rani met Rohan, an employee of the same call centre in which she works. Their friendship because deeper. One day, Rani invited Rohan for dinner in her flat. In order to please Rohan to the core, she cooked food very carefully. She wore a skirt and a top. She hid the teddy bear and the poster of the earth. She hid mini in her bedroom.

Rohan was talking about politics and Mini was smiling. She was agreeing on every point of Rohan. When Rohan said that keeping pets inside flats is not good and that pets can remain much happier if they are kept in the environment outside a flat, Rani supported him. When Rohan said that he wanted to take Rani to a disco bar, she gave her approval in a Jiffy. Rani does not like going to discotheques. When Rohan praised her dress, she said that a person's dress must reflect his or her inner personal ability and that she wears this type of dress so that the woman inside her may be reflected.

Now, a question was cropping up in Rani's mind. She was saying those very things that she never believed in. Was Rani speaking in reality? But Rani was sure that if she disagreed with Rohan, or if she told Rohan that she would part company with her cat, or if she expressed clearly that she does not like to go to disco bar, or if she bluntly said that she does not like wearing skirt, Rohan would start disliking her.

Without any pressure on her mind, Rani had decided how she would behave with him to please him. She also defined some rules in which she fully took care of the things that Rohan would like and not like. Hence, she thought it better to hide her real personality. She never thought even once that she was good the way she actually was.

Rani's story is just like those of other people. They are something else in their real life. Their behaviour becomes something else in their dealings with others. That's because they worry about what others would think. They fear that people would be angry with them.

Paradoxical Aspect of Personality

Besides, there are some other people whose personality is in mutual conflict. Their personality is different at work place. There personality is totally different at home. Both these types of personality are not their real personality.

But they do not know how to control their behaviour at both the places (work place and home).

We are appending an example here.

Mahendra, a middle-aged man, appears to be a very dominant and clear, outspoken man at home. He can tell, while watching a cricket match on TV, which team would win. He can take the government to task because of the latter's wrong policies. He expresses his opinion with anger even as he watches news on TV. He has clear plans for his two children. He talks to his wife for many hours regarding bringing up his children. If he gets a chance, he meets the teachers of his children (in school), and he gives them a piece or two of advice to them as well.

When he returns from his office, he is very tired. He looses his temper over small issues. Hence, when he reaches home, all members of the family become cautious to the core. They take full care, lest he should quickly fly into a rage.

When he reaches office, Mahendra changes completely. He never says anything to anyone forcefully or in a coercive manner. When his advice is sought for solving a problem, he tried to defer the issue. When he is told to say something in a meeting, he tries to say something (after thoroughly analyzing the issue) which the organizer should like. He always has work more than his capacity. But he continues to work even after office hours to complete work instead of requesting to reduce its quantum or asking for an aide to give him support. That is why he is very much tired when he comes home and does not have enough time to spend with his family.

Mahendra is among those persons who are trapped in the paradox of their life. Due to this paradox, he is troubled. He knows that he love his family and so, he does not want to hurt his family members. But when he returns from office, he is unable to control himself. Nevertheless, he remains struck with terror and suppressed in his office.

Those, who are nobler and gentle than they should be, may have to face many serious problems due to this personality that is full of paradox. At his work place, the fear of losing his job keeps Mahendra worried beyond compare. At home, he tries to release his worries by the wrong means. That's why his family members remain afraid of him.

Sometimes, it so happens that a person does not get an opportunity to express his emotional experiences. In such a situation, he tries to express such emotional experiences in a wrong manner in some other part of his life. If Mahendra's colleagues come to meet him at his home and see how offensive he is in his family setting, they would be shocked. Similarly, if his family members see that he works in office in a fearful manner, they would also be surprised.

Mahendra feels that the change in his behaviour at these two places is not something for which he is accountable to anybody. That's because he does not have control over his behavior. He puts forth the logic that he knows that his behaviour is not normal. He cannot change his behaviour only if he is aware of its abnormal feature; it is not a likely possibility.

Please Do Not be Angry

Nidhi, like the other people of the world, is irritated by people in her immediate vicinity at some points of time. She is a married woman of 50 years of age. She works for a private firm. Nidhi does not let anyone know that she is quite bothered from her inside. She never complains to the person due to who she is in a troubled state.

She talks to other people to relieve her mental burden. She tells them her tale of woes. If she is fed up of her husband, she tells her friend about it. If she is bothered by her boss, she tells her colleague about the issue. If she is troubled by her mother-in-law, she tells her husband about her agonies. The people around here are peeved listeners. But the person, due to who she is agonized, never learns that she has some kind of grudge about him or her in her mind.

Nidhi fears that condition the most when she thinks that her near and dear ones may not learn that she has been tortured by them. She thinks that the person in question would feel hurt. He or she may reprimand Nidhi or treat her badly. She is certainly fearful that people would be angry with him. Besides, she is also afraid of the fact the people do not like to listen to the critique passed on them. That is why she narrates her fearful stories to Tom, Dick and Harry but does not share her feelings with the actual person—the real culprit. But no one is able to learn that he himself or she herself is also a source of his agony.

Her friend tells her that she should talk to her husband. In reply, Nidhi says, "I cannot do so. He is busy in office throughout the day. When he comes home, he would not like to listen to my grievances." Her colleagues give the advice that she ought to talk to her boss. But she responds, "I can't do so. He would get dozens of employees like me. I don't want to lose my job."

Thus, this chain of events continues. Nidhi is afraid that if she criticizes the behaviour of a person in his or her presence, he or she would be angry with her (Nidhi). We know that she knows how to express her emotional experiences. That's because she has always been doing so. But she is not able to display the right behaviour in front of the rightly concerned person. There are many other people like Nidhi who are expects in stating what's in their mind but cannot complain about the behaviour of a particular person by looking into his or her eyes. This is an example of delusive impulse.

It can never be resolved. Due to it the feeling of suffocation keeps on increasing inside the person.

I Am Like That Only, I Can't Say 'No' to Anyone

Ravi loves to work in a stealthy manner. He avoids becoming a centre of attraction. When he is at work, he tries not to be seen or spotted by anyone.

In some facets of his task, Ravi is just perfect. He is the regional sales manager of a firm. His behavior with his customers and employees is very good. He is decent and wise. He can listen to the complaints of people with unlimited patience. He often finds effective solutions of the problems presented by people to him. People like Ravi. They think that he is a fine man and that he can do anything for them.

But Ravi is never able to come up to expectations of his employer. His employer and senior officials see him mixing up well with people. That's why they are not able to comprehend why he remains silent in meetings. Why does he not give suggestions? Why does he not take the initiative? They are unable to understand that if Ravi can remove the complaints of his customers with high speed and agility, why he cannot do good commercial deals with his stubborn suppliers? Although employees love him, he is unable to keep them disciplined. Why is that so? Why are his sales figures not as impressive as those of other sales managers? Other managers do not deal in such a friendly manner with their customers and office employees, just like Ravi does.

His seniors think of giving him a promotion. But they think that he lacks the requisite virtue. They say that the virtue he lacks is called determination and ambition. But Ravi knows that there is no dearth of determination and ambition in him. The only thing is that he does not like to say 'No!' He does not want to become a bad man in the eyes of other people. He does not want to give bad news to other people. He thinks that if he says 'No,' other people would mind his refusal.

He does not try to understand that although the employees like him, they also misuse his weakness. Similarly, suppliers also take him for a ride, for he is very gentle and cannot refuse. They know that he would never refuse to accept or do anything.

Thus, due to the gentleness of Ravi, his employees can face dilemma, people like Ravi can be in much deep kinds of dilemma. People like Ravi do everything to make themselves ideal people. Their bosses identify their virtues and since they are impressed, they employ them. But their bosses also expect them to have 'spine.' People like Ravi do not possess 'spine.'

Ravi wants to be liked by everyone, so he never irritates any one. He does not feel that if he gives some terms and conditions or directives (related to official work) to his vendors or employees of firm, this act would not make vendors and employees angry. Rather, the opposite would happen. They all would think, "He is harsh yet he is truthful." One can say this about those people who maintain a balance in these two aspects.

Child-like Behaviour

Raju and Leena have formed a successful married couple. They are young Leena teaches in a private school. She does not have any difficulty in controlling naughty children. She is happy passing time in the company of children. When she returns home from school, she is not at all tired. Rather, she acquires enthusiasm from the task of teaching (in school) and thus remains enthusiastic at home.

Raju is a government employee. Contrary to the popular opinion, he also does consider his job to be boring and full of dullness. The department for which he works makes new plans and implements them. That way, Raju takes the plan process as a challenge. Thus, he also returns home with loads of energy.

Raju and Leena fight at home quite often. These conflict-oriented situations do not last long. Both share the experiences of each other, they also tell about their individual achievements. Their enthusiastic style, youthfulness, the spirit of brave heart, some good friends and the determination to accept new challenges always keeps them busy.

This happens most of the times. But the question of parents arises, this does not happen. Both have a special type of attachment. Both love their parents. Both depend upon their parents in emotional terms. The parents of both live in suburban towns that are nearby.

When the festivals like Holi and Deepawali are near, Leena and Raju are bothered beyond limits. The parents of both Leena and Raju think that they should come to them on the festive occasion. But it becomes difficult for Raju and Leena to go to one township first and then, to another township. Thus, when the festivals are near, they are worried. They cannot celebrate the festival according to their wishes, for they may face a guilt complex if they choose to do so.

This does not happen during festival days alone. The parents of both of them want them to spend Sundays with them. In order to avoid this trouble, Raju and Leena switch off their telephones or cell phones. They make the programme for Sunday in total secrecy. They tell their respective parents that they both are busy on Sunday.

For many people, it is very difficult to behave in a

proper manner with either parent or both parents. They think that they cannot properly face their parents or any one of them. They go through some emotional experiences during their childhood years. When they become adults, the same emotional experiences (or feeling) continue to dominate them. Thus, they start behaving with their parents in a childish manner. They take special care of the reactions that their parents would give about their behavior. In some cases, the behaviour of such people can be according to the expectations of their parents. But in most cases, they behave according to their own opinions and beliefs. They are so much struck with terror that they do not try to form their independent opinion. They do not muster enough courage to speak against their parents.

Such people try to maintain this unique type of destructive status quo. Due to this, they remain suppressed and subdued. The people, who prove to be having strong determination in their daily life, may find that such a situation may be full of lassitude for them. Besides, due to this type of paradox, feelings of delusion and anger are born.

I Have No Importance

Very noble people have a special symptom—their self-confidence and self-respect are weak. They feel why any person would like to be their friend. That's why whenever they make a relationship with others, they consider themselves to be of nil importance to deal with others.

They feel that in order to satisfy other people and also, to get the praise of all, they should always keep on doing something. Let us study the example that follows:

Mukesh works at a high post in a private firm. He is not at the top but he is above the middle level of management. He himself does not know how he reached such a high position (in his firm) because he does not have faith in his own ability. He thinks that he knows what other people demand. He provides them his services. That's why he has probably got this cushy post. Or, he knows very well now he can convince people that he can do a lot many things.

When he is told—he may not be told either—he takes the responsibility of doing additional work. He changes his busy daily schedules and works according to the requests of others. That way, he has to face the wrath of his friends and kin.

He knows that due to his typical nature, other people misuse him. He is also irritated beyond compare due to this very reason. But he is always afraid that if he would not obey others, his friends would leave him and also, he would lose his job. Even if he thinks about telling someone, he starts having a guilt complex. This is a word that is uttered by mouth with great difficulty. HE is terrified because he thinks that people might criticize him. That's because he believes in presenting himself as a perfect gentleman in front of people so that his impression may be good on all of them.

He knows that he can lead a life in a better manner as well. He evaluates his friendship from time to time. He thinks that if he stops accepting the commands of all people, his friends would leave him. He becomes panicky even by the thought of leading life without his friends.

That's why he defers the process of self-analysis. That's because he remains doubtful that if he changes the already established system (and norms), his life would be surrounded by hardships.

People love him because of his basic personality but he does not want to accept this fact. His friends like his lively, brave heart—like nature. They like his constructive attitude. They appreciate his knowledge about current affairs. His colleagues trust him. They know that he can easily handle most stubborn customers quite successfully, a task that's not so easy for others.

Mukesh is one from among those people who are unable to see their own selves quite clearly. They agree with the statements of all other people who interact with them.

Ones, Who See This World with the Spectacle of Nobility

If you are very much noble and show a very highly noble behavioural pattern, you are not easily ready to accept that many people do not behave like you. In other words, you consider that giving preference to others and dealing carefully with people is quite 'natural' and 'correct'. That's why, you aver, you do not like to listen to any statement or logic against your this notion. You may be shocked to learn that other people do not behave like you. The reality is that your life becomes full of treachery, deception, anger mixed with agony. Due to this, your life becomes a store house of lassitude and frustration.

The reality is that some people are unable to decide what the right word really is. Thus, their mind remains uncertain about such subjects. Some people do not bother at all about what other people would think about them. Some people do not care for the sentiments of others while hurting or bothering others. The number of those persons is very high who do not edit their thought properly and those who do not bother about what type of reaction people would give to their thoughts and emotions. Even if they think that it is necessary to bother about the feelings of others, even then they are not hesitant while stating or doing what they want to state or do. Some people are experts in getting their work done.

You know very well that a time comes when you are

not able to see this world with the spectacle of a gentleman. There is also an occasion when they do not think much; nor do they care for the result.

When noble people are hurt by a statement or act, they always do not believe that they have been deliberately irritated, bothered or hurt. The realm of their thinking has no notion of this type. So, they are not easily prepared to believe. The noble people, who have a narrow viewpoint about the world, believe that other people must know that their behaviour hurts and causes dejection. That's why they must be behaving in that manner due to their helplessness.

Gentle people think that all people of this world must think according to them only. They think that all people must behave like them on, and they also think that all others must feel like them only. They think that all people should also be sensitive like them only.

Thus, when they find that the rest of the world is not like that, they are in trouble. They do not take off their spectacle. They expect that the world would behave with them according to their nature. That way, they make themselves ready for getting hurt (by the world) once again.

This truth is not that simple. The number of those people is not less who do not believe in doing welfare beyond a limit. They don't even know that you can have any problem. That's because they look at the world from their own view point and are unable to understand that if they do not have any difficulty in saying anything, how can others have difficulty? Probably, they find it difficult to imagine that there can be a method that is different from their own.

For some people from among you, worse situations can arise. When such bothering circumstances come before you time and again—and you think that it is happening deliberately—the fact is corroborated that you have been living in a Utopian world. You receive the bashing, the wounds, and start arriving at the conclusion that your importance is nil.

What we want to say, can be understood with the help of an example that follows:

Ashish works for an MNC. There is part of a safety and health committee in his firm; he is one of the eight members of that committee. A review meeting is organized twice a year. In this meeting, the implementation of the firm's directives is reviewed. It is recommended that members organize it only during free hours.

But Ashish and his colleagues are very busy. So, they find it difficult to fix a date for meeting by consensus. When Ashish is responsible for fixing the date, he sends messages to other committee members over telephone and via e-mail. He tells them to attend the meeting at a time when is convenient for all of them. He has to waste additional time to do so. But he wants that all should be happy with his alacrity. So, makes special efforts to help all.

Such meetings are organized turn by turn. When Ashish is not responsible for coordinating the proceedings of the meeting, the story is different. Three members of the committee sit together, decide what decision is to be taken and then, they inform all members about the meeting date. Other members must take time out for the meeting by any means.

Since Ashish would never like to organize the meeting this way, he would not believe that other members can also do such an act. He does not consider it appropriate. He thinks that the reason behind this act that his colleagues are not serious about his busy schedules are he thinks, they must be considering him a man of nil importance or a useless person.

What is the right method of organizing such meetings?

Ashish thinks that his method is correct. When his colleagues organize the meeting according to their way, he considers himself to be useless and of nil importance (since his advice is not sought). On the other hand, hi colleagues think that their method is correct. They think that someone has to take a decision, and then, everyone must be informed. They think that they cannot afford to waste time on fixing dates. It doesn't matter who is right, for no method is correct.

Here, the most important thing is the opinion of Ashish. Due to this opinion or notion, he becomes peevish. He also starts believing that he is not important for others. Such a narrow viewpoint about the external world gives setback to his self-confidence.

It's Important to Identify Paradoxes

If there are some facets of your life that are fine and you also like them, paradox can naturally put you in a fix. "Why do I perform my best but become helpless in front of people?" "I am adept at developing relationships with people but why do I become pathetic and meek in front of my parents?" "I am very much courageous in front of my beloved but why I become so weak in front of my boss?"

Such a person is difficult to find who had never faced paradox in his life. It is difficult to find a person every aspect of whose life is fully balanced or fully unbalanced. Many people feel that their lifetime has been wasted but the reality can be opposite to this. When someone is not very much bothered and does not face serious mental problems, it is impossible to become the best in all facets of life, even if anyone claims that he or she can.

On the basis of evaluation appended in this chapter, you can identify paradox and look at the problem in the correct perspective.

Where is your sensitivity focused? Which facets of your

life do you know about in which you would be behaving in the same manner under similar conditions? Which facets of your life would you like to change? Which facets of your life do you consider to be impossible to change?

The first important step for bringing about permanent change is—increase your awareness. The better you understand what you do, under what conditions you do it and with which people you do it, the stronger desire you would be able to develop to change.

It is important to note that when you behave on your own, you take hours, days or even weeks to find out the reality. In such conditions, a reaction comes out from your inside. It is not much connected to your nature that you are not able to understand that you are doing so.

Your first challenge is—try to understand your subconscious behaviour at least once and accept that this happens. Another suggestion, for your practice, is that you should count the number of times when you say, "I am sorry," and there was no need to do so.

The next stage is—focus on those moments when a strong desire swells within you to do something different but you are not able to do it. These are the moments when the brain says 'No' but your mouth utters 'Yes.' While speaking 'Yes,' you feel that you are sans energy.

Then, identify those moments when you lose your self-control (either internally or externally). Whatever is emitted out of your mouth, cannot be controlled by you. In order to increase awareness, it is important for you to identify the reason behind the anger, and it should also be seen what you were not able to express clearly during the last few days or weeks. Then, you should observe, whether this feeling of petulance continued to accumulate.

At this point, it is not important to do anything in this context. Increasing your awareness would be an important step for you. That's because that way, your view point would be clearly formed about what you do and when.

Am I Unbalanced?

When you understand that due to your behaviour, your life has been limited inside a small circle, it means that there is one weakness or the other. This can be the lack of humour feeling or continuity. It can be your style of living under the shadow of fear. Due to this, you may be feeling that your life is not able to move on the right track. It can be your style of living for others due to which you are not able to save time for you at all.

If your life is limited to such a type of circle, the feelings of lassitude, emptiness and hopelessness would keep on increasing inside you.

Then, what is the meaning of being finely balanced?

We can consider ourselves to be fully balanced when your internal world – it includes your thoughts, emotional experiences, ambitions, desires and dreams – is fully compatible with your external world. If there is a wide gorge between the internal and external worlds, balanced would not be established. The mean of "being properly balanced" is – your external behaviour finely reflects your internal emotional experiences and expectations.

You can feel sometimes that you are leading secret life but at the same time, you are displaying a different type of behaviour in the external world. Your secret world is constructed through those conversations that you imagine about. Alternatively, you do so according to the outline of ideal behaviour in your mind. It is constructed through those unstated impulses that continue to accumulate due to insult, injury, anger, selfishness, desire and expectations.

Every person has his secret world of mind. This is an important part of the identification of his independent personality and existence. But in very 'noble' persons, their real personality is hidden often due to fear. This inner personality can also be like a chameleon. You can give it the colours of your immediate environment (so that no one's attention may go to it). You do so when you try to chisel your personality according to the will of others. That way, there is no coordination left between internal and external worlds.

When you yourself control the feeling of 'nobility,' not leaving it on the mercy of fear and worry, the distance between your internal and external worlds would continue to reduce. That way, your true personality would start getting revealed.

4

You Are Not Born with Civility

Whatever may be your age, you feel that your behaviour is a natural part of your existence. The colour of your eyes, shape of your hand and feet also are a natural part of your existence according to the same logic. It is difficult to imagine that you may have been different (sometimes in your past) from now what you are. We think, "I am like that only." We may not like it. We may be thinking during the moments of introspection, "I wish I could behave in a different way!" But despite this, we think that we did not have any alternative. We are like that only.

This is not the truth. We are not like what we had always been. You continued to become like this. You were not born with gentlemanliness. When you were born, you needs were—milk, clothes, sleep, sitting in lap etc. You were able to express lucidly whatever you demanded. You used o cry sometimes because you wanted to cry due to no reason.

Look at a child carefully. You may be having children. Your family (kin) may have children. Your friend's child can be observed. If you have not observed the daily routine of a child carefully, you must have done so on TV or in movies.

Children are not decent, noble guys. When they need something, they cry. They know about their need in a clear way. They do not know how to speak but they know what they want. They do not hesitate to give adequate hints (or gestures) to tell what they need.

Some children cry a lot; some others cry too little. Some

children are naughty and some others are calm. All children know what they need. They use their personal methods to convey their need to their parents. So, they cry, smile or look with anger. They want to drink milk, change wet clothes, play, remain alone, remain awake or sleep. They want to play with others, or they like to be contained within their own selves.

Children do not think about the results of behaviour. They do not bother that their behavior can cause trouble to someone. They do not care if someone is angry with them. They do not bother about the reactions of others. They are not doubtful about the criticism being showered on them. They do not bother whether their behaviour is appropriate.

They do not think about the result while raising a hue and cry. They love to do this. They do not think, "Should I do this? May be, people would dislike me!" You were also self-centred at one point of time. But did you learn that when you don't like a thing, how you should say No?

But during the process of highly necessary socialization, another process had been going on. You had been learning that some parts of your behaviour are not acceptable. If they continued to remain as such, it means that you would be deprived of love, acceptance, recognition etc.

Besides, you may have been praised because you had become gentle, you had kept your mouth shut, you had obeyed orders or you may have been treading the oft-treaded path. You must have learnt how to become additionally sensitive towards the needs of other people so that you may be able to get love and acceptance. "I am like that only." This is, in a way, a statement for revealing the lack of power in you. Most noble people feel this. But the notion "Here, I am built" reflects the understanding that how you changed your own self and now, you are in a position to do something in this context.

In this chapter, we shall discuss what had happened. Why did you become too much good or noble?

Golden Era of Rearing

There is no such era in the past, nor is there any such era in the present. Further, the era in which we live now, would never come back. The golden era of rearing is an imagination which we do not realize on a general basis.

In this chapter, the conclusions of insufficient and negligent rearing have been pondered over. Our goal is not to hold parents wrong or guilty; no such effort has been made in this text. Nor do we want to nurture the feeling of sadness by recalling the events of our childhood.

We expect that you would make god use of this opportunity and correctly identify the origin of your present behaviour. There is no use of leveling allegations, nor is it appropriate to consider ourselves guilty. That's because if you do so, you would be more agonized than before. But when you learn why you behave in a particular manner, you would be able to see your problem in a correct perspective. Then, you would be able to do anything for its treatment.

Parents are not bad; there can be only a few exceptions to this rule. In sum, too much noble, gentle people are built not because of bad parents but because of wrong rearing (of children). Further, wrong rearing is also not always responsible. We see many people around us whose parents love them. They take care of them. But many times, their affectionate behaviour became so much illogical, sans perseverance and careless that its adverse effect was received by children.

Rearing has always been a tough job. There are many responsibilities in this process. One has to make a lot of efforts; and work is never finished. Parents have to use patience while bringing up their children. But no one gives training about how to rear children. It is believed that "This would be done automatically." The women, who become pregnant for the first time, have to listen to these sermons, which are useless.

If you are doing a job, you are getting salary in lien of it. Thus, you must have taken special training in the context of your occupation. People doing self-service also get some type of training. If you do not take training, your manager does give you clear directives and guidelines regarding your job. There must be many among you who must be undertaking the responsibility of training others.

The information about a new disease is gathered. For example, AIDS was brought to the notice of the world. Imagine what kinds of problem doctors, nurses and scientists had to face when AIDS was revealed as a killer disease. A new machine or computer is installed. Do we already have al technical knowledge? No! In most cases, when a new thing is started, it is not publicized in advance. For that, we need to get proper training.

But the same thing is not applicable to parents. In most cases, some tips of advice are given by doctors. Some others are given by friends and kin, and the same are deemed to be the guidance. In modern society, the trend of nuclear families is growing at a fast pace. In such times, the cooperation and support of the seniors and elders of the family is becoming a tale of the past.

Thus, parents are not able to understand clearly how the newly born member of their family should be reared and looked after. Modern mothers buy books on parenthood from markets and read them. But we know that such books are full of such sets of information as are in conflict with one another. After reading these books, the confusion of these new mothers can increase.

What do parents do then? They try o take the best steps on their level. But their best methods are not the best ones at all times. And after becoming adult, you suffer because you were not guided properly in your childhood.

What Really Happens?

Parents alone are not novices, insofar as rearing and taking care of children is the issue. Rather, in most cases, children also have the anarchical nature. There is a need to work very hard on them to make them part of society and also, to make them decent and better human beings. Children are stubborn, naughty, clever and always keen to test the patience of their elders. They are absorbed in their own selves. They use their skills to get their work done (or demand fulfilled). They know very well how they can attract the attention of their parents towards their own selves. They know how to manipulate their parents to grind their own axe. Parents cannot bow before their demands at all points of time. That's because if they do so, their children can become.

In every society and family, there are methods of making children decent and courteous. In order to make them responsible citizens of their society, these children are taught some special qualities. This means that they are taught about the need to establish dialogue. They are also taught to get their thoughts and desires accepted (by others). They are taught to behave according to the socially recognized patterns. They are given good sets of knowledge about such (social) behavioural patterns. These patterns are recognized by society. One can become part of society only after learning and following such (social) behavioural patterns.

You are taught how you should use folk and knife at

the dining table even as you take meal. You are taught how to use toilet. You are taught what types of clothes you ought to wear and how you should tie your shoe laces. You are taught about etiquette. When elders are taking, children should not interrupt the talk by speaking. You are taught how to say "thank you" to someone and how to wish them. You are also taught that the feet of elders are to be touched (with hands). You are taught that you must not criticize anyone in his absence and that you must not tell lies. You must not steal things or money. You must avoid being greedy.... And so on. Similarly, you are also trained about religious rituals (of your society and religion).

If all these things are not taught at a certain level (to the child), the child gets an environment in which it becomes possible for him or her to perpetuate the state of anarchy. Sometimes, they can tread the paths of crime and thus become the unwanted elements (at a later stage). In the absence of the right type of training, children are unable to understand this world, even though they grow up. Thus, they are not able to behave properly.

The problem takes birth from this point itself. The responsibility of adults is to make children decent. But this process itself cannot be executed in a correct manner. Due to their mistakes and frustration, parents threaten their children, reprimand them, abuse them, criticize them, make fun of them and exploit them in emotional terms. They torture children in many types of psychological and physical way. They do all this so that children may learn to behave according to their will. Such an imposed behaviour hurts the dignity of children. Thus, their self-pride and self-confidence are weakened.

You must have met such a child as may have made you angry because of his * behaviour. You must have wished to reprimand such a child.

This is the result of teaching and training children in the wrong way. Then, parents are unable to find a good solution for rectifying their child. Mostly, such parents have also to tolerate bad experiences in their own childhood years, and they try to repeat those very experiences with their children. Nevertheless, many parents can be found who would state that whatever behaviour they had been given during their childhood would not be repeated with their own children. But till the time they do not become aware of their own behaviour and do not learn the exact formulae of bringing up children, they would remain the slaves of their old habits, or they would be busy making a few new rules.

On the other hand, if children are anarchical and insolent, they are also good-natured, honest, creative, curious and full of social nature. Their willpower is strong and they are fully dedicated towards their goal. Very strong blows are not needed to put an end to their lively nature and prosperity; nor are very bad behaviour needed to put an end to their energy and curiosity. That is because children are little as well as sensitive.

Similarly, parents do not have to exert heavily on children to take them in a direction in which they (the parents) want them (the children) to go. Parents threaten you, make you feel scared, look down upon you. Thus, you become obedient children that way.

Quite often you take a decision, "I shall not do that again." The chances are less that you would cross the defined line because your mind remains fearful of the reprimand that you would be given (by your parents). If such type of discipline is used at a general level, the emotional development of children would not be hurt. Rather, children would be influenced, up to an extent, due to this kind of pressure.

When a person was a little kid, his parents used to repeat time and again, "Had I been in your place, I would never have done that." Or, they used to tell him, "You would not be able to succeed." Parents loved their child and that's why they used to say so. They used to utter these words because they did not want their child to fail. But when the child would try to do a new task, his brain used to reverberate with the sermons given by his parents. Thus, his self-confidence would start shaking.

When he grew up, he started facing failure in all tasks that he took up. Be that job, his own enterprise, friendship, relationships with kin, he failed. The fear of failure also started affecting his married life. Thus, his children also started getting affected.

Were his parents bad? No! They said all this because of the lack of knowledge.

We are appending ahead the examples of behavioural patterns through which the children are dealt with nowadays.

- The number of those children is high who are thrashed every day. Many of them are locked up in room for many hours.
- An adopted child is threatened that if he did not mind his habits, he would be sent back to the orphanage (from where he had been brought).
- A little girl was told by her mother that her father might die due to her rudeness. Her father was a heart patient. She was told that she would be held responsible for the death of her father.
- The parents of one child used to tie him up with rope so that he could not more here and there and create mischief (when they were away, in their respective offices).

- Many children are threatened, if they create mischief of any kind. They are told that they would be t hrown on the road.
- In some families, parents mock at their child when he talks to a third person.
- In many families, the child is gagged when the angry gaze of his or her father falls on him or her.
- In many families, children are made to feel scared through the tales or threats of ghosts or by using tantric rituals (on such children).
- Many parents give wrong punishment to their children. Later, in order to justify their punishment, they state. "We are doing this for the sake of your welfare only."

Making Children decent is the desire and need of parents. It is not the desire or need of children to become decent.

A long list of the bad behaviours of this type can be prepared. But at this point of time, it is important to remind you that you must also have faced one or more of the aforementioned behavioural patterns. Your parents must also have tried to make you civilized by using one method or the other. How do you recall your childhood? Are your memories clear? Have they faded?

It is not important that you were treated in a cruel manner in your childhood days and it may have deeply affected your emotional growth. If unrealistic expectations are imposed on you in your childhood days, the impact of being weak and incapable remains in you even after you become an adult. It is not necessary that you were thrashed with a stick or you were reprimanded and coaxed consistently so that you might change your habit.

If you are told time and again that you are not handsome

(or beautiful), or if someone tells you that you would not be able to succeed in sports, or if someone comments that you are lazy, or if a person avers that your nose is skewed, or if someone tells you that you ask to many questions, you can be adversely affected (by one, a few or all of these questions).

For example, when you sang in a poor manner or made a dirty painting in your childhood, such incidents affected your personality deeply and seriously. This deep influence continues to grip your personality. You can take a decision not to sing again or not to paint again.

There must be many aspects of your life towards which you may plausibly be very sensitive. There is a complete possibility that the root of those facets is connected to your childhood (when something happens to you or when you are told something). In such cases, how can you trace the origin of your behaviour?

If you are unable to recognize that origin, it does not matter. The memory of every person is of a different type. Some people are able to remember even those events that had occurred in their life at the age of one year. Some others have only hazy memories of such incidents in their mind. Some others do not remember anything—for them, their initial years of childhood are like a big zero. Try o recall whatever you can.

If you wish, you can ask your brothers and sisters. You can talk to your kin. What are their memories regarding your childhood? The memories of brothers and sister can be different from those that you have in your mind.

If you are unable to recall a particular incident of your childhood, even then it is a fact that the talk of parents for insulting in childhood or for hurting (in the childhood) remain in your memory for a long period.

You Do Not Have Any Will

A complex facet of good, noble behaviour is that sometimes, you do not know what you want. You go so much away from your emotional experiences and desires that you are unable to understand your wishes. Thus, you are cut off from your real wishes. This is a result of wrong rearing (on part of your parents); your wishes were negated and eschewed when you had expressed them.

Let us read an example.

On a bus stop, a bothered mother was standing along with her five-year-old daughter. She was wearing a beautiful frock. She had a birthday gift in her hands. She said, "I shall not attend the birthday party of Nishita." I don't like her."

"No! Don't do this. You like Nishita. She is your best friend. I don't want to listen to anything else. You must go there."

"She is very bad, mommy. I hate her. I don't want to see her face. I shall not go."

"I won't listen to this rubbish. The bus has arrived. Come along. Nishita's family likes you. You must come along."

When the mother looked at her daughter in such an angry manner, the people standing at the bust stop started staring at her.

A tired mother was taking her daughter to attend the birthday of her daughter's friend. The daughter was creating a scene at the pubic place—it was a spot where her mother had never expected her daughter to oppose in any way. All children know how to protest. They know what would be the right time to become stubborn (to get their terms accepted) and thus, they act accordingly.

This does not mean that the lady in this example is a

bad mother. But she was sending a message to the subconscious mind of her daughter. The message was that the daughter's notion or thinking was not correct. She said to the daughter that she (daughter) liked Nishita. But in reality, her daughter did not like Nishita. She told her daughter that the family members of Nishita liked her. But the child does not like to go to the residence of Nishita. The most confusing thing in the girl's mind was that she was being forced to believe in the thing in which she did not have any belief.

Had her mother desired, she could have used limitless patience to persuade the girl. She could have bowed before the child. Thus, she could have said, "What's it, daughter? I was thinking that you like Nishita. Tell you mummy, what's wrong?" In most cases, children want that the elders should listen to their mind's thoughts and also, they should give importance to such thoughts. In That case, a way is found through which concord is reached between parents and child. But here, if the opinion of the girl is not being considered, she is being forced to accept such a thing as she does not want to agree upon.

After this kind of scene, this child would not feel what is wrong. However, her conscious mind would be affected. She would recall that scene time and again. She would recall how her mother had forced her to go to Nishita's residence. It is just possible that she may cry throughout the day after reaching Nishita's home. She may throw objects here and there at Nishita's home and that way, she may try to express her suppressed emotional experiences.

Let us study another example. You must have witnessed such examples in your daily life.

"I need an ice-cream."

"No, you don't need it."

"I need it. I want to have an ice-cream."

"I have told you—you don't need it."

"I want it. I want it. I want to have an ice-cream."

"I have told you—you do not need ice-cream. Now, stop behaving like a spoiled child and go to your room."

Such a kind of scene can linger on for quite some time. The end of it could be the crying or subbing of the child in question. He is in a fix. He wants to have an ice-cream. But he has been told that he does not need it. To an extent, this episode may appear to be normal. Parents do not want their child to eat ice-cream, so they are refusing to buy the same for him.

But in fact, it is not a normal thing. People can say in a different manner as well, as follows.

"I need an ice-cream."

"I know that you need an ice-cream but I do not want you to eat it. That's because we shall have dinner soon."

"But I need it. I need one only."

"I know that you need one only. But I am not going to buy it for you, not even a single one."

This kind of discussion can go on for some time. Children are naturally stubborn. IN the end, the child can cry or sob. The difference is that there would not be the generation of a feeling of confusion in the mind of the child. He would not get the thing he demands but at least, he is told about the reason behind the denial. Thus, he does not a wrong meaning (in his mind).

If you were not given the things you wanted to have in your childhood days, you would find it very difficult to be clear about your desires in your adulthood years. Can you recall an incident when you were told that you do not want to have a thing but in reality you wanted to have it?

Can you remember how you had felt at that time?

It's No Use Crying Over Every Issue

You were told that you did not want to have a certain thing. But you did want to have that thing. Besides, you were also plausibly told that you were not feeling something weird. But you knew that you were feeling that way. It happens only when an adult is unable to face the tears of a child.

Due to the sobbing tactic of the child, he unsolved problems of the adult can be highlighted. Thus, the adults can think that they are bad parents because they are unable to protect themselves from the shock.

An adult can say to stop a child's sobbing, "If you stop sobbing, I would give you something." Or, he can say, "It does not look nice to cry over everything." Or, he can aver, "Good boys do not cry." Or, he can say, "You have grow up but still, you are crying!"

None of these things proves to be effective in a special way. But these things do affect the emotional experiences of the child. If you are not permitted to feel what you are feeling, this can prove to be harmful for you. In such cases, there is the generation of a feeling of confusion in the mind due to desire. Besides, all this happens for the benefit of the adult, not for the benefit of the children. Adults say so to avoid the inconvenient feelings or experiences.

During the course of Olympic Games (1996), one such incident of denial had been witnessed. The player associated with that incident was not a little girl. But it can be considered to be an example worth emulating.

This had happened in the final round of the event of female gymnastics. A participant of the USA had lost her balance and slipped. Then, it had been declared by authorities that she was not eligible to win gold medal or any other medal in the competition. She came out of the ground. She was crying due to agony, lassitude and shame. Her coach came forward to console her. The cameras and microphones were focused on the player and her coach. They did not bother about the privacy of those two persons. The entire world was watching this on TV, the girl was crying bitterly.

The coach caressed her back and said, "No problem. Your team shall win the medal nevertheless." These consoling words of the coach proved to be effective. The coach had used a special style to tell this to the player, he was able to communicate to her that he was able to comprehend her emotional experiences.

Parents become helpless when they see that their children are sad and agonized. They say many things about which they do not think carefully. For a child immersed in his own emotional experiences, the talk of parents seems to be confusing and misleading. Parents want to tell (through hints and gestures) that the emotional experiences of children are not correct.

This does not happen under those circumstances alone in which children cry. Many parents censure their children by stating, "He is too sensitive." Thus, they negate the emotional experiences of the child. The peak of that impulse is weird, many children are forced to feel stifled or secluded, for they are unable to express their impulses properly.

In many families, emotional experiences are banned. The family members are taught to keep mum. Can such a sermon be given to a newly born child? Some children try to do even this. They are so much miffed or peeved at the regular crying of their child that they try to give a hint to the child that crying is a bad thing.

Crying is not at all bad. All people know that a child

uses crying and sobbing to convey his needs and desires to others (parents), whereas the children (especially boys) are persuaded through crying. They are even told that they are doing this to win sympathy. Tears also have a fixed objective. But when we see some adults who have very effectively destroyed their emotional experiences, we start wondering whether these people have dried up their tears forever!

Tears are said to be the indicators of shame. They are considered to be the indicators of man's weakness and hence, shameful for any man. IT is said that men never cry and that only women cry. Tears are deemed to be unwanted and negative comments are passed about them. But the reality is that tears are the best mode for expressing one's emotional experiences.

What do you think about yourself? Can you recall an episode in which your negative experiences were defied, or when you were told that you should feel (or not feel) in a particular way? Are there some rules prevalent in your family regarding emotions? Are emotions respected in your family? Or, all they negated and censured in your family? Are they laughed at? Or, are they understood?

What kind of result (of negative desires and emotional experiences) can come to the fore when you become an adult? If you are asked what your need or desire is, or if you are asked what your emotional experiences are, you would probably reply, "I do not know." Generally, deep in your heart, you do know. But when you keep o listening to the definitions of emotional experiences of other people, you may start feeling that the emotional experiences may be impossible to bring out of the deepest core of your mind and express them in front of others.

If you say what your desire is, you may be criticized. Hence, you would say that you do not have any desire.

Do you think that you have some people in your life who can tell what your desire is? Some people are expert in telling what other people desire. Without any doubt, generally, they tell about your desire and thus push the responsibility towards you. If, during the course of your rearing, your emotional experiences are negated, it becomes easy for others to impose their desires on you.

We can understand this with the help of an example.

In a departmental store, a lady was purchasing goods along with her three-year-old daughter. They had a trolley to put things in. The mother took the trolley and her daughter towards a rack in which biscuit pockets had been arranged. She asked her daughter, "Which biscuit do you need?" The little girl pointed out towards one particular packet and said, "This one." The mother said, "No, you do not need that. You need this, for your father likes it." She picked another packet and put it in the trolley. If the mother was not supposed to buy the biscuit packet demanded by her daughter, why did she ask her at all?

If such types of incident occur during the course of your rearing, when you would be asked, in your adulthood, whether you need a particular thing, you would start thinking whether you really need that thing. Clever people would say, "What is your requirement?" Thus, you would believe them. You would think that whatever thing they deem to be apt for you, would be fine for you. But no one else can know about your real needs better than you yourself.

Read the following examples.

A woman's husband – she has already divorced him – used to tell her that she loved him very deeply; and the woman thought that since he was overemphasizing this statement, he must be correct in stating it.

A man married at the time when he did not want to marry. But he had believed his beloved's statement that he loved her from the deepest core of her heart and that he wanted to marry her.

A person does not like to apply for promotion in his office because his colleague says that he does not need to do a job. Thus, his determination starts wavering.

A woman went to spend her vacations along with her friend to a specified location simply because her friend liked that location. This woman did not have any intention whatsoever to visit that location.

Some people feel that they really do not know what they want or how they feel. They find it very difficult to take a decision, for they feel that whatever they would think may not necessarily reflect their need. They forget the habit of identifying their mistakes and thus start searching for similar possibilities.

There is no dearth of people who know, from the core of their heart, that their needs and desires are suppressed. But they are afraid of presenting them. So, they say, "I do not know." Or, they aver, "Whatever you say would be fine with me." Or, they would state, "It does not matter. I would accept whatever has been decided." They never state, "I want that." They never say, "I feel that..."

The first thing—how do you recognize your needs and desires? The second thing is—are you able to express your needs and desires so that they may be fulfilled or accepted?

I Am Doing This for Your Welfare Only

Have you ever heard such a sentence before? This is absolutely false.

There are many things that people do for US in our life and that are certainly for our welfare. You must be having pleasant memories. You must have the incidents in your memory in which liberalism, compassion, cooperation, sympathy and cordiality were used by your parents and other elders to contribute effectively towards your welfare.

But it is the truth that when you are little and another adult tells you that he is doing something for your welfare, you should become careful. This invariably means that they are serving you to grind their own axe, no for your welfare. This generally means that they motivate you to change your behaviour and adopt a new behavioural pattern for the sake of their own convenience. They do not do so to make you a social creature.

When adult people are not able to tune with your basic nature (in your life), they start imposing rules and regulations on you. They also start giving you sermons. Your different nature is not the reason but they are unable to digest your nature. It is not that your behaviour resembles that of angels in your childhood years. But generally, when parents are not able to comprehend what to do next, the child has to suffer and become experienced.

If such a thing has happened to you, the most suspenseful situation must have occurred when your life is full of happiness and only then, the anger of your parents comes like a storm (in your life). Then, a fear comes into your innocent mind.

And when they start doing this to you, you start changing your behaviour due to your desire of being accepted by others. It happens when an additional understanding is generated in you like a razor. Through it, you select the right type of behaviour for yourself (so that everything may remain fine). You keep on thinking in your conscious and subconscious mind, "On which issue would my parents be angry with me?" "What should I do?" You would think. You would also think, "What kind of expectations they have from me?" Finally, you may also think, "How should I behave?"

When you are pretty young, it is not necessary that thoughts may be coming up in the form of words in your mind. They are only experiences of emotions you can give shape to. Alternatively, you can be punished. The meaning of punishment is being divested of love, affiliation, acceptance and recognition. These things are necessary for the child so that he may feel safe and secure.

When you were little, you must have changed your behaviour to adapt yourself to the needs of parents (and other adults). Their needs must have been changing continuously over time. But you must have tried to guess what they wanted. You must have failed to make such a type of guess. The base was not certain and the power to change the rule was in the hand of someone else. It may be possible that there were different rules for every day or week and the conformance to such rules may have been difficult for a little child.

This means that you were being forced to live under fear. You were nurturing the fear that your parents might not become dissatisfied or angry with you. This means that you used to make your environment full of fear to protect yourself from the plausible anger (of your parents and elders).

That is why the feeling of imposing the environment started growing and becoming strong inside you. It catches the signals of even a small problem so that there should not be any problem. So, they start searching for solutions. For a small child, this action is no less than punishment. You must have tried to cheer up your parents upon seeing that they were sad. You must have done something to please them.

Even then, it is not easy to please them. Every time, you have to be careful and think where they would strike the next time.

Failure is certain. Every little child cannot remain alert at all times. He may have irritated his parents even if he did not want to.

But habits are consolidated through practice. You get many opportunities to adopt the habit of becoming a different person. You find out what is the best and most acceptable method of learning the behaviour that is expected from you. Thus, in a bid to change or would yourself according to the other person, you forget your real personality.

And while talking about all this, you miraculously save your own self. You learn some easy and fixed procedures to avoid changing rules, targets, inconvenience and conflicts; you had gone through them during your childhood days.

How We Assimilate

We are trying to tell how children change your natural behaviour to win the heart of their parents and how they acquire new behavioural patterns. It is possible that one or more methods (procedures) may appear to be familiar to you. Such a behaviour may not be useful to you now. Bu you must have drawn good help from this type of behaviour to overcome your moments of crisis. During the period of those crises, that behaviour must have been compulsory for you.

These methods of adopting behaviour are also the representatives of some special features of your personality, and they can be against your personality acquired by birth. In this list, the various types of personality and also, those methods of protection have been included which you must have invented to protect your own self. We have mentioned some fixed types of behaviour separately; these are adopted by 'noble' children. We have also given a title to such types of behavior. But it is not that a person is always attached to only one type of behavior.

Rather, you entire personality is built due to the integration of your virtues, conduct, habits and practice.

Here, many types of behaviour and methods of protection have been analyzed. On the basis of that analysis, you can understand the special type of method that was developed by you in your childhood years. The objective of this analysis is not to do any medical examination. Rather, its aim is to present a model on the basis of which broad possibilities may be discussed.

Here, the thought, "I am the one who pleases others" is not operational; nor is the thought, "I am self-centred" operational here. Rather, this list would help you understand that when you natural and true behaviour was not accepted in the environment in which you were reared, what type of behaviour you had adopted to save yourself.

When you look back and review how you had adopted the new type of behaviour, you would realize that your behaviour was also different at different times. Sometimes, you used to take proper care. Then, you would try o get the peaceful settlement done. A time must have come when you must have felt ashamed. On some occasions, you must have been fully free from such behavioural patterns and you must have used these behavioural patterns at one point of time.

Good Child

Good children are really good. They understand the message quickly that if they do good work, they would be patted on their back. The meaning of correct work is that whatever tasks parents may give, these (good) children rarely file a complaint for the inconvenience caused to them. Their clothes are not very dirty. They follow all rules of the present. They never bother their parents.

Such children invariably remain secluded in their own self. They would themselves in this form. They never want anyone to be angry with them over any issue. They remain silent, and they can think that a storm can hit their life. Although silence is visible inside, there is always a possibility (of the arrival of a storm).

When a child gets the title of "Good Child," it is difficult to separate it from the child. That is because it is always expected from them that they would always remain 'good.'

Peace Messengers

Such types of child are always in favour of maintaining peace. They try to sort out the disputes between their parents. They also try to bring amity between the relations of two siblings and being them on friendly terms. They are always peaceful. They eat shoddy, dry food. They can tell about the qualities of any TV programme, book or person, these are the qualities towards which the attention of other people is not diverted. These children do not like their talk or suggestions to be discarded. So, they do not like if they are disagreed upon.

They do not like to argue like a child. In order to avoid the conflict, such children can spend their entire strength. If everything is not fine, even then they would state that everything is fine. They would never accept the opposition to the statement (or opinion) that life is the name of a peaceful and felicitous passage.

Obedient

These children are like good children. But they have the habit of living under the shadow of extreme fear. They are fully alert towards the concept that their mistake should not be caught. Nevertheless, obedient children are not naughty. Even then, they are afraid that they may be considered to be naughty.

They also believe in following the rules properly. They are so much determined in this context that they delineate rules at such levels (to follow all rules) as are harsher as compared to the rules defined at the family level.

Children Who Satisfy People

Such children are always on the lookout for stating an exact statement to please the adults around them, or, they try to do a fine job and show it to the adults.

The behaviour of such children is pleasing, they are clever too. They spend most of their time in guessing what types of expectations the adults would have from them. Before the adults demand an item, these children would arrange the same.

Guilty Child

This child thinks that he is at fault in everything. Such children presume that they are squarely responsible for whatever wrong is happening around them, so they are guilty. That is why such children are not able to remain happy. They are not able to play. They keep on sitting in a melancholic, silent state, for they are terrified by the hurry that due to them, adults should not face any difficult. They also admit that whatever they would do, they would commit mistakes, or they feel that their work would lead to botheration for others.

Shameful Child

These children are like guilty children. But they give importance to "what they do and what else they are beyond that." The children, who are ashamed of themselves, really believe that something wrong is inside them. They keep on asking for forgiveness for no reason.

Critical

Such children label other children as 'bad' and thus, they themselves try to project their own selves as 'good.' They look for vices in others and report about those vices to their parents and teachers very quickly. They try to become better in the eyes of the world. But they consider it necessary to pull the legs of others to do so.

Taking Care

Such children take special care of their siblings and parents. In fact, they learn to take care of things (and people). Such children make themselves highly useful. Thus, parents mostly trust such children. They are accountable beyond the normal need. When they grow up, they consider it necessary to do additional tasks and participate in various activities. That's because they believe in helping others.

Such children become busy in solving the problems of other people (after growing up to become adults). They may or may not get a reward for their efforts but they do solve the problems of others.

Tending to be Self-dependent

Such children do not have to be looked after. Whenever attention is focused on them, it seems that they are capable of handling the difficulties around them to such an extent that parents have a sign of relief. They think that they do not have to worry about at least one of their children.

Strong children do not show their weaknesses, or they do not express their soft feelings. And it is believed that they are not influenced, unlike other children, who are easily influenced due to their emotions and passion.

Passive Child

If a child remains bent and struck with terror, he becomes passive. He becomes passive if he does not attract the attention of others. What do you want to do? How you can do this? In the context of these two questions, you become so much dependent upon the will of others that it becomes impossible for you to express dissent. That's because you do not have courage and energy left in you to express dissent.

Passive children are very pragmatic and street-smart. They can change their own selves according to the needs of the present as and when they want to.

Absent Child

In the language of psychology, it is called "Being Absent." For some children, the problems of real life are so much that they find a way to get rid of their worry and fear. In order to do so, they separate themselves from the process of the present. Whatever is happening to them, their body remains present during the course of that process. But they become absent in psychological and emotional terms. They shrink inside their inner shell to such an extent that no one is able to touch them.

In case of children, who are sexually exploited, we can see this very frequently. Besides, some children use this method to protect themselves from such parents as always. Yell, reprimand and coax them. Such children do not pay attention to the impromptu words coming out of the mouth of parents.

If a child is rarely reprimanded, he learns from this kind of reprimand that such a treatment is also effective. But if a child is reprimanded at all times and it is said that he is in the wrong, he can totally separate his mental word from his present to protect himself.

They would smile and say, "Yes, Yes! It's alright mummy. Ok." But in reality, they are not paying attention to the talk. For them, listening to others (elders) about their limitations and weak points is a painful experience. Hence, they ignore such types of talk.

Habit of Hiding

All children tell lies; and all of them hide things as well as do a bit of acting. This is a natural part of building an entity – the thoughts and emotional experiences should be the ones about which others may not be able to know. This happens during the process of separatism and also during the process of developing the identity of the self and this happens quite naturally. When a habit of this type is developed, you start using falsehood to protect yourself from the anger of your parents and teachers. Most of the children – they may be noble or not – want to use falsehood.

But the habit of telling lies and hiding things of noble children adopts a new form. They become expert in hiding their emotional experiences and thoughts so that no one is able to understand what kind of hullabaloo is going on in their inner self. They know how to hide their emotional experiences in an effective manner so that people may consider them to be righteous (even if they may not be righteous in their inner self).

They tell lies and hide things because they feel ashamed of what they are. They feel that the thoughts and feelings they have are not with other people. Hence, they hide them in their own selves so that they may be able to avoid being mocked at or feeling ashamed.

Ineffective

The meaning of 'ineffective' is – gelling of all types of emotional experience inside our own selves. Hence, emotional experiences are there but they are obstructed.

In fact, children find many problems while expressing emotional experiences. Thus, they try to make their own selves ineffective in emotional terms so that they may not feel the agony.

Creation of the Image of Parents in Inner Self

It has a miraculous effect. After some days, parents do not have to give any advice. They give negative messages to their children in such an effective manner that children put those messages (sermons) of their parents in their heart and brain forever.

Upon growing, they become such persons that when they do anything, they do not ponder over its good or bad facets. Rather, they start criticizing their own selves. Thus, they say, "You are such a big fool. You are of no use. You cannot do anything." Thus, they think on these lines. They do develop a habit of reprimanding their own selves.

If you recognize that the image of your parents is imprinted on your inner self, it means that you have also a fully adopted their reprimanding style in your own self. The only difference is that the voice is yours. But you can always censure your own self whenever you wish to do so. You can also censure your own self for your ineptness, foolishness and ignorance.

The gist of all these things is that the brain of elder overpowers the young shoulders that you have (due to your young age).

Noble children grow up quickly. They start thinking like adults well in time, they start behaving like adults too. In order to do the right piece of work, they keep a sharp vigil on the activities of adults and that way, they start behaving like adults.

They are not able to enjoy their early days (of childhood) since they are always worried, bothered or doubtful. They do not want to take any wrong step. If they feel that their parents can be angry, they restrict their needs and desires. They become so much habitual of suppressing and negating their natural emotional experiences that they become ripe (mature) before the due time.

You Have Alternatives

As you grow up, you try to adopt such behaviours through your own methods (so that people around you are not bothered). Thus, you are not born with those qualities but you make such qualities a part of your behaviour due to your own liking.

You can counter the logic by saying "What kind of alternative can a child of two years possess?" You can also say, "How can a child of seven or ten years of age select the right kind of behaviour?"

In fact, the question of selecting does not arise at a young age. Then, we do not think that way. "Good! I have many alternatives available. Now, I am not able to understand which one is to be selected. I can choose what my mummy likes. Or, I can choose what my papa prefers. Or, I can choose something my mind approves of. "Although it may seem weird listening to this, the opportunity to select is available at that time also. Some children do not show their choice, unlike others. There must be children in your own family. Who would not show the choice that may be somewhat similar to yours?

There is the control of the fears of some results on your choice. You always have the fear that you would lose something and due to this, you may feel unsecure or unsafe. That's why you decide to imbibe the behaviour of others to protect yourself from becoming insecure.

Since adult people (like our parents, other relatives, teachers and others) make rules of this type, we do not have many alternatives in front of us. We are unable to feel that we can have other alternatives too.

An exercise is being appended ahead. You can understand the process of selection with its help.

Exercise for Alternative Practice 1

You go back, down your memory lane, to the maximum possible extent. Try to recall when you had decided to change your behaviour with complete awareness because you had felt, after thinking about its results, that doing such a thing would be a sign of wisdom. At that time, you had deliberately brought about change in your coveted work. And you had done something that you had not liked to do.

Or, you try to recall an incident that was shameful, troublesome or agonizing and after which you had deliberately changed your behaviour (so that you may not have fee the agony or go through a similar trouble come experience again).

It is possible that your parents had a conflict and you might have thought that they were fighting because of your mistake. Then, you might have decided that you would not say any such thing in the future due to which your parents could fight against each other. It is possible that in your class (in school), you were insulted in front of all your classmates. It is possible that when you were playing, an adult had pointed out that your behaviour was 'bad.'

Your age was less at that time but you must have succeeded in assessing the circumstance and visualizing the results of tasks (at that time, in the past). After that, you must have thought carefully and brought about change in your behaviour. Your brain was not capable of understanding the results, so you must have done away with one behavioural pattern and selected another alternative behavioural pattern. That way, you must chosen the best behaviour—you selected that evil out of the two evils that less lethal.

Although many alternatives may have been available for many among you but you must have felt that you do not have any alternative.

When Selection Becomes a Habit

In your childhood years, you may have selected alternatives after fixed intervals of time. You must have faced new challenges every day, every week or every month. Then, you must have pondered over the problem and selected an alternative behaviour for yourself.

You must have seen what would be safest and most apt behaviour (under the situation you were in). And while doing so, you must not have felt that you were selecting the behaviour by becoming fully alert. After some days, you had become such an expert in doing away with your old behaviour and adopting a new one that the changed (new) behaviour had become the identification of your real personality.

In the first statements, it has been said, "I am like that only." You take up alternative as a habit. When you do so, your natural behaviour is moulded accordingly.

A system of structure construction remains inside man. This is good that it is there. For us, it is not necessary that we should learn how to do only one task from the scratch by doing it time and again. Our brain becomes accustomed to the revival or revision of all types of stimuli. When we work incessantly, we keep on learning.

As has already been stated, it is easy to force a child to learn a special type of behaviour by making him scared, threatening him, making fun of him or insulting him. When the child has to face the situation on a continuous basis, he quickly learns to change the behaviour (so that he may not have to go through an unpleasant circumstance). We learn such types of experience only through habit. We ought to learn a few lessons in the childhood years to protect our own selves.

Rules of Traffic

In every city and society, children are taught how to cross roads by educating them about traffic rules and traffic signals. Why? Since children do not know properly about traffic, they cannot Judge that a mishap can occur. Only adults have the information about this.

Children are unable to understand the equation between distance and speed. Parents and teachers understand this. So, they teach their children the rules related to traffic because they are worried about the safety of their children (when the latter are in traffic).

Children are taught: "Look towards your right before crossing the road. Then, look towards your left. If no vehicle is visible, cross the road by taking swift steps. Do not run." This is a very useful rule. It is put in the little brain of children time and again. Thus, children learn this rule that way. After that, whenever they try to cross the road, this rule continues to overpower them.

All of you must have learnt traffic rules in your childhood days. With the help of these rules, roads can be crossed safely. Later, you continue to follow those rules.

Till the time you do not grow up and till the time you do not understand the intricacies of traffic, you feel that there can be other alternatives for crossing roads. When you become wise, you feel that all rules, taught in your childhood years, should be followed with dedication. Then, you change your habit.

But it is more difficult to change an emotional habit.

When you see a car coming towards you, you can tell yourself, "The speed of this car is not so high. Before it comes close to me, I shall walk across the road and cross it." Thus, you take a decision in a Jiffy and cross the road by running across it. But when you face internal emotional pressure instead of external traffic, you are unable to break that habit. In life, the emotional types of alternative are difficult to choose form vis.-a-vis. the alternatives presented to you in your life.

Alternative Practice Exercise 2

Recall an incident that had happened in your immediate past, when you were aware and knew that you were supposed to do a particular task. When the time to select a task arrived, you did another task. What happened? Did you ponder over the selection of an alternative? Did you talk about it? Did you yourself think about it? In the end, how did you select a totally different task?

Now, go to Alternative Practice Exercise 1 in which you were supposed to select an alternative with full awareness (but you were a child at that time). Is there any similarity between these two? Are the emotional experiences connected with both of them different? And the most important thing is—do you feel that in fact, there was no alternative in front of you?

Hence, it is important for us to get rid of emotional pressure and habits.

●

5

Change in Behaviour is Possible

If you want to change your life, the fear of result can come before you as a challenge. You think that the results would be lethal. But this does not happen in reality. Only your opinion makes you feel afraid.

In most situations, too noble people show a reaction. This reaction is very high vis.-a-vis. a fixed required value. This happens when our brain wants to say 'No' but our mouth says 'Yes.' That's why there is a long discussion or debate in our brain. We look for the best answer and fight against our own selves. And we are not able to say anything to our own selves.

Fear of Result

On one side, the thought of stating the exact thoughts flashes across our brain. When someone says something to US, we are peeved which is our reaction to his talk. Or, when we want to yell, "This is not correct," Our impulses reach the battleground and they take the control of our brain in their hands. In such a situation, we lose the capacity to state what we want to.

Instead, we become crippled, or we are reluctant, or we speak exactly opposite to the answer lying in our brain. We are terrified by thinking about the results that would pour in if we speak whatever we think. We feel that we shall be thrown out of the job, or our spouse would leave us, or our parents or other kin would never forgive us, or our dearest friends would not like to have a linkage with us.

We imagine that we shall hurt the feelings of the other person. We imagine that other people would consider us to be stupid, sans thoughts, harsh, rough, heartless, selfish or pitiable. We imagine that other people would not be able to accept us. We think that they would laugh at us or insult us. Alternatively, they would be angry with us. Since we lead life in a subdued, suppressed manner and always accept bad conditions, we are ready to do anything to stop that (negative) result from pouring in. Thus, we avoid saying what ought to be said.

Whatever is there, it is a type of emotional and imaginary world. The imagination about the bad result does not allow us to see the situation clearly. In our mind, excessive emotional experiences start blocking the rational, logical way of behaviour (as a reaction to whatever is happening).

Then, we are unable to give our reaction in an effective and natural way since the fear of result over powers us. This fear keeps us in chains. We feel that we are incapable of changing this uncomfortable situation, for we had already imagined that whatever we think or feel, should not be uttered because doing so would lead to the generation of bad results.

Now, it is possible that while reading these lines, you may state, "But it may be possible to do this." You can give any example in this context. You may tell how you had to quit your job, or how your beloved left you, or how your aunt stopped talking to you. You can recall any such incident in which you had said what was in your heart and someone's eyes had starting rolling out tears.

Yes, you are right. It is impossible. Many times, weird things happen. Many times, in the worst probable event, we are kept as a central character. Many times, we are reprimanded, insulted, rejected or left to drown in a sea of lassitude. Many times, we are left on our own. We are ignored. While promotion is being given to others, we are not considered. We are censured in our absence. But too noble people always live under the shadow of the fear that they would have to face bad result only.

In this book, it has been mentioned how we develop the capacity to assimilate to protect our own selves during our childhood years. We also start preparing after 'smelling' the danger in advance. The same child, who was always alert to remain safe, works inside us even when we grow up to become adults.

Hence, a special type of alert nature is developed inside us. It always remains alert to feel the potential danger. This means – remaining alert for dealing with an incident that may happen. In this incident, eschewing shame, languor and injury would be an ideal choice. This means we keep on thinking what is going to happen and what the possible results can be.

For an excessively noble person, maintaining this type of thinking is normal thing. "I am like that only." Due to the thoughts like this, the number of possibilities is reduced, in terms of number, in your life. That's because you take a decisions about the result much earlier. When you act and behave in a defensive manner to protect yourself from the potential dangers, you would be painfully entangled in worry and botheration.

Such a type of defensive behaviour kills your natural nature. It closes the doors of your capacity and kills your perseverance. The worst thing that transpires is when you are not armed with your natural qualities. Then, when the opportunity arrives, you are not able to face lethal outcomes in an effective manner. Rather, you spend most of your time in worrying about what is going to happen in the future. In the meantime, you also lose your natural capacity to handle difficult circumstances. This means that whenever you react with the feelings of fear and suspicion, your emotional resources start reducing.

At one level, this paradox seems o be complete. If you are fully alert, your emotional experiences would warn you about the danger that is coming and so, you would be able to deal with all dangers in an effective manner. But this does not happen in reality.

During this period, what happens is that your nicely woven emotional reaction comes to the fore which continues to repeat itself in every new situation. In your mind, the experience remains; it is full of insult of the result of the past. That's why you are not able to give your reaction in a natural way. But if you continue to express your reaction on the basis of the experiences of the past, it would not be possible to clearly see the circumstance of the present.

Many times, we think that we can remain alert to face all possible emotional problems. But this is not possible. What were the alternatives in front of us under such circumstances? We can take our attention away from them and focus on new circumstances. That can be a right method.

Let us study an example.

Anamika is a yoga teacher. She goes to the home of people and teaches them yoga. She ekes out a living for her family by earning fee from her clients. Her nature is good, so she has to face many difficulties every now and then. She cannot demand money from her clients at the end of the month. Not only this, if a client joins her class late in a yoga training programme, she spends additional one hour to train him, and she does not charge any fee for imparting training in that extra period.

When Anamika was a little girl her nature had become so because the ruling member of her family had terrified and terrorized her. She was sent to hostel at the age of three years. In the hostel, order children used to dominate and rule. She used to fear that she might be punished or rejected if she opposed the norms there. So, she had adopted the nature of noble girl. So that she may not face difficulties.

The real problem is that in childhood years, fear overpowers the mind of the child. This fear does not leave the person even when he or she becomes an adult. In other issues, Anamika did not face any problem but in professional issues, her self-confidence used to shake.

Overtly, it was easy for friends to say, "What's your problem? Ask for money from clients at the right time. This is the money earned by you after doing hard work." Covertly, it was a difficult task for Anamika to ask for money. That was because the rules that she had adopted in her childhood years could be broken if she asked for money from her clients. She was dealing with her clients in the same manner which she used while dealing with the head of the family (who used to dictate terms to her.) That means the supremacy of fear had been established in her mind.

The emotional experiences of Anamika were the real experiences for her. She needed to deal with the fear of emotional experiences (with her clients). Her clients were not likely to scare her away in any condition. They used to take time in paying fee because Anamika never demanded money from them. She never used to ask for money the additional hours spent on their training. Her customers were misusing her but they were not bad.

The fear of result is one half part of the equation. It obstructs natural qualities. The second part of the equation is a follows:

First of All, Imagination Is Done. Then, It Is Assumed to be True

To an extent, most people create an imaginary picture about a situation in their brain. Then, they start assuming that the picture is true. Too much gentle people evaluate a situation on the basis of the fear of result. Then, they select a behaviour. They also believe that it is true.

Let us read another example.

Subhashini is a 35-year-old woman. She is the only daughter of her parents. Her parents have grown old. She works in a good company at a high post. She has been warding off marriage proposals by stating that she does not have time for marriage. She says that she would think about marriage after one or two years. She works in a big city and lives alone. Her parents live in a small city. She goes to meet her parents on two Sundays in a month. She loves to spend holidays with her parents. She has other hobbies as well. She also has some (female) friends.

Every year, Neena, the friend of Subhashini and a married woman, invites Subhashini to spend the New Year Day with her. The family of Neena is large. This family lives in a hill town. Subhashini loves to visit that town and the family of Neena.

But every year, Subhashini refuses to come in the New Year Day's party. She says that if she did not give support and comfort to her parents on the New Year Day, they would feel bad. That's because her parents prepare a lot to celebrate the New Year Day. Her mother cooks food of her choice on that day. Neena gave many types of logic. She said to Subhashini, "If you do not visit your parents. This time, if is not going to matter. You spend two days in a month along with them. Your parents won't feel bad about it. Why don't you ask them and get their opinion?"

But no, the sound of dissent starts taking birth in the mind of Subhashini. Her parents are getting old by the day. It is just possible that this year's party may be the last one of their life. They depend so much upon you.

Once, Neena and her husband forced Subhashini to attend the New Year Day party in any case. They said that if she did not attend the party, Neena would end her years old friendship with her.

Now, Subhashini was on the horns of a dilemma. On one side, there was an invitation of her friend which Subhashini wanted to accept. On the other hand, she was worried about her parents. She knew that they would mind it if she did not remain in their company on the New Year Day. She talked to Neena and other friends over phone for several hours. She told them that she was facing a dilemma. She used all types of logic. But her friends held her responsible for this dilemma.

All of them advised her that she could ask her parents and get permission from them to go to Neena's place. "I cannot do this. They would think that I do not want to be in their company on the New Year Day. Thus, they would feel bad about it."

Finally, Subhashini came under all types of pressure. Thus, she asked her parents (before the New Year Day, on a Sunday) that she was being invited by her friend on the next New Year Day party. If she went to meet her friend, Subhashini asked, would her parents be bothered on any account? If they would be, she could change her decision, for nothing had been decided yet.

What was the reaction of her parents? They said, "We have always been wondering why a young girl like you has been celebrating the New Year Day party in our company. You should have decided to join your friend on the occasion years ago. We are pleased when you are with us but we also want that you continue to meet your friends."

For so many years, Subhashini stopped herself from attending the celebration of New Year Day that was done every year at Neena's home. That was because she feared that if she did not stay with her parents on that occasion, her parents might feel bad about it. In fact, she had already recorded or imagined the probable reaction of her parents in her mind (well in advance). She had been taking the decision (to reject the invitation of Neena) on the basis of that very imagination.

Subhashini and limited her alternatives because she had convinced her own self that her opinion was correct. She had not asked for the advice of her parents even once (on this issue).

Let us read another example.

Raju is a young salesman. He is enthusiastic and ambitious. That's why he gets a good salary at the shop where he works. The shop deals in electric goods. The owner of the shop loves his enthusiasm and dealing method (with clients).

On the other hand, when Raju meets a person who is smarter and better than him, he is bothered. His master—the shop owner—is an example in this context.

He believes in moving ahead. Thus, he thinks about only one way—he must keep his master pleased and avoid committing any type of mistake. Sohanlal, his master, came to him and asked him if he could stay at the shop for extra hours. Raju said that he would be pleased to stay for extra hours, for he does not have any busy schedule for the evening.

Next week, he was again told to stay at shop for extra time. He was told to help the owner in preparing accounts.

Then, Raju said that he would not be troubled if he stayed on. Thus, this system continued. Thus, Raju had to stay for one day or even more (for extra hours) at the shop. Raju's friends asked him what amount he was getting as overtime. He used to reply that he had never asked for the wages in lieu of overtime. He used to tell them that he was working late because it was his job to do work at the shop. His friends would not be convinced by his logic.

He faced the problem for the first time when he could not attend the birthday party of his friend. Now, Raju feel troubled. He could not promise to anyone, for his master could tell him to stay on in the shop at any point of time.

Time passed. Raju noticed that his friends never used to invite him for a gathering or party. He asked them the reason behind this. They told him that there was no point in inviting him, for he had failed to join such gatherings but stating, at the last moment, that he had work to do at the shop.

Raju's troubles increased in terms of number when he became the friend of a girl and started taking her out. The girl praised him because he was ambitious. She also accepted that the time of meeting could be changed because he could be told to work in late hours at the shop. But when this system lingered on, the girl felt that everything is not fine with Raju.

"You have been doing work in overtime hours for the past six months and not getting money in lieu of it. This is your stupidity. At least, you can ask for a pay raise or enhancement of your status."

"I cannot do that. Had Sohanlal wished to increase salary, he would certainly have done so by now. He wants me to be present at the shop during late hours. If I refuse to do so, he would appoint anyone from among the scores of unemployed boys roaming here."

"What are you talking? You can demand this from him. If you demand, he would not throw you out. You can also understand this."

"No! If I do so, he can misunderstand me. Then, he would not like me at all. Even otherwise, he does not talk to me with openness. There is always an expression of anger on his face."

Raju also knows what his master is thinking. He also knows what he is going to do. He has already made an imaginary picture of the entire situation in his mind. How does he know all this? He has never talked to Sohanlal about pay raise. He has never expressed his dissent over the issue of staying at the shop during later hours.

He is living in a situation of extreme caution. He has already told about bad outcomes and he is presuming that his master keeps on thinking about him and he also knows what his master thinks about him. Thus, Raju is doing this job by keeping all these illusions in his mind. He does not demand the money in lieu of the overtime work, for he feels that working in overtime (without monetary reward) is his duty. He thinks that if he demands money for the work done in overtime, he would be thrown out. He has also imagined that his master does not like him and so, he does not try to express his dissent.

Due to the effect of the fear inside him, Raju was never able to think that his master could also be happy by employing an energetic employee like him. Raju learns the intricacies of business and works very hard to do so. He is a clever businessman and if Raju is working hard, he gets happiness due o this. The master is presuming that till the time Raju does not demand a pay raise, he would not increase his salary. But he has decided that on the occasion of Deepawali, he would give Lefty bonus to Raju. In fact, he likes Raju and wants him to work for him for a long duration. He does now know that Raju thinks that his master does not like him. Raju thinks that his master is always angry whereas most colleagues of Raju know that since their master is always busy, he is always serious.

Raju followed the advice of his beloved. He talked to his master one day. Then, he realized how much wrong his notions were. Had he remained in this dilemma for a long period and not talked to his master, he would have decided to do away with his job. Then, he would not have learnt what type of imaginary image he had made in his mind. The reality was exactly opposite to what he had been thinking.

The conclusion is that when you imagine and start behaving on the basis of your wrong notions, your brain creates a deceptive situation. Such a situation can be dangerous for you.

In order to get rid of this problem, it is important for you to see from the viewpoint of others as well. Your thoughts are your own. Others can examine your thoughts and give a non-biased opinion about it. Then, you can analyze your own thought on the basis of the suggestions and opinions given by others.

Looking at the problem in that way may seem to be complicated for you. Your unstable brain reflects your present view point. It also tests the discussion held by you with another person on the testing parameter of fear. At that time, it does consider it necessary to focus on reality.

If we become afraid of the result that would come after listening to others' opinions, we should certainly be overpowered by worry and botheration. Too much noble people do not pay attention to alternatives. They always have to bear the excessive pressure of their brain.

Identify Your Emotional Experiences

As has already been discussed, every person assimilates good behaviour in his special style. Hence, every person gives his reaction in a different manner in different situations. By reading the incidents mentioned in this book, you can feel that some tendencies are already known to you. But your emotional experiences are your own and your behaviour is also your own.

Here, we have tried to tell you how emotional experiences can be identified. When you behave in a noble manner, the emotional experiences being generated in your mind, your thoughts and physical reaction are such as have been described earlier. Two simple exercises are being appended here. You can identify the emotional experiences of that type with the help of these exercises.

Good/Bad Practice Exercise 1

Before you begin, ponder over the reaction you have given upon reading the heeding.

You can do this exercise alone or in the company of other people. You may or may not be acquainted with them. Since everything is going to happen in your brain. If you are alone, imagine that you are sitting between two persons. They can any two persons—such people whom you may or may not know. If you are going by bus, or if you are sitting in an office, look at the people sitting or standing near you. The idea is—there must be two persons in your brain, one person on each one of your sides.

You may be alone or among people. Now, you have to think that you are going to say a good thing to the person sitting on your left. You imagine that you are praising him in a low tone. Observe carefully—how do you feel? Was it so easy for you to praise someone? Did you think something and then, you changed your mind (to decide that you would not say it? That was probably because you felt that if say that in a loud voice, that person would not trust you. If you have the opportunity, write down about the emotional experiences cropping up in your mind.

Now, imagine about the person sitting on your left side. Think that you must say something evil to him. In other words, you have to insult him. Imagine that you are talking to him direct at a high pitch of voice. Note what the reaction on you was. Did you feel hesitation? Did you ponder over many words and then changed your mind and decided not to utter those words because it was not possible to say so? Are you thinking, "What a lousy practice exercise this is! I am being told to become a bad man. I am being incited to insult another person."? You may think, "I can't say such a thing to anyone." Do you think that way? What's the purpose of saying this?" Do you think, "I can't think about saying something bad to a person whom I do not know"? Or, you say, "I cannot say anything bad to an acquaintance at any point of time." Did you imagine about many bad things, considering this to be a game and thought that in reality, you do not have to say anything?

Then, if that's possible, write about your experiences. Are you feeling that you have cramps in your stomach? When you were imagining about saying anything bad, was your face shining with a smile? Were you keen not to speak at all? Probably, through this practice, you must undertake a kind of mental journey. Did your throat dry up and did you feel that you had been told to say a very weird thing? Did you become happy upon getting the thought of saying something insulting (to another person)?

Did you make a long list of those reasons which described why you should not do the practice exercise? Were you rectifying those things in your mind which you considered to be necessary or not necessary, or the things (talk) that could hurt someone, or the things (talk) that could be safe?

Were you imagining about your own reactions? Did you imagine that the other person would have become angry? Don't you think that he would have felt hurt, full of languor?

Did you ever imagine that the other person could have attacked you in verbal, even physical terms (given that you had offended him)? Did you imagine that the other person was shocked beyond compare or that he was insulted very deeply? Whatever physical, emotional and mental processes you could feel then, jot them down on a sheet of paper.

Good/Bad Practice Exercise No. 2

Recall an incident of the past in your brain in which someone had said something to you. As a result, you were bothered. You became angry or dejected but still, you could not do anything. Alternatively, you accepted that behaviour. You thought that it could have been your mistake and that the other person could be right. Probably, you were not able to do anything at that very moment.

Recall—where were you at that moment? What clothes you and other people had worn? If other people were also present there, where were you in physical term? Was it day or night? While recalling that incident in your mind, you must be thinking that you could not speak up what you had in your brain, and you could not speak up because you were too noble.

Had your heartbeat increased? Was your throat dry? Did you have stomach ache? Were you overtly laughing, despite the fact that you were deeply agonized from your inside? Were you feeling any kind of hesitation from your inside? Had you said something stupid or baseless? Had you thought that the behaviour of the other person (towards you) was correct because it was so because of your mistake (in any form)? Had your eyes become blank for a few moments? Had you not been able to understand what was happening? Were you seeing the ground while going back?

Was this one of those circumstances that you had thought about the other person and behaved with him by considering it to be true? Had you imagined that if you told what you wanted to tell, what would the other man think? If possible, Jot down all these emotional experiences. Did you ever feel yourself to be sad, dejected, unarmed and weak?

Now, go back to the scene. Imagine that you are saying all those things that you really wanted to say. By telling what you felt, your heart may feel relieved and light. Thus, you can feel ecstatic. But did you have that feeling of ecstasy? Had you said to yourself, "I can never do this"? How do you imagine that if you tell the real truth of your heart to another person, what would be his reaction?

When you identify what had happened to you, compare with the list when you had imagined that you would say something bad to someone. Do you find any similarity in these two? Do all of your reactions match one another in all circumstances? Are they totally different?

What Has Happened to You?

When you would be practicing like this, your brain would be reacting in many ways. Many types of emotional experience dominate us and we feel that they alone control us, not vice-versa. Our logical brain knows what we should do to protect ourselves. It knows how we ought to be looked after, whereas our emotions continue to dominate us. Our emotions mostly want to rule over us, in sharp contrast with our desires.

When you are in such a situation (in which you do not know what ought to be done), it becomes necessary to find out what has happened to you. Now, what you think should happen to your own self or what do you want to transpire but is not transpiring.

We do not say that you become a bad man or start saying bad things (about others). Then, you would become opposite to what you are. The objective of presenting these two exercises is that you should be able to identify your physical and emotional reactions during tough circumstances.

But the very thought (that you have said something bad to someone) produces uncomfortable emotional experiences in you. Then, it is a clear sign that you have remained a noble man beyond limit for a petty long period. Real circumstances do not bother you. Rather, you are bothered by just thinking about them.

Till the time you don't know what your behaviour is, you cannot do anything to change it. All types of physical, emotional and ideological reactions tell what you do. You can take the first step with awareness by monitoring your behaviour (to change in an effective manner).

The list of the behavioural responses of people has been appended ahead:

- Smiling
- Hesitating
- A desire to cry
- Clapping
- Shaking a foot
- Not looking into the eyes
- Feeling shy
- Coughing

- Feeling stomach ache
- Being unable to think
- Feeling hotness in the body
- Shaking or moving
- Staggering
- Laughing by becoming nervous
- Hiding face
- Having a dry throat
- Chewing finger with teeth
- Feeling as if passing out
- Becoming talkative
- Shaking head
- Staring at the floor.

Mostly, you use the language of your body and communicate your message to others; that way, you tell that you are in an uncomfortable state. Although you think that you have succeeded in hiding your internal upheaval, your body's language tells an entirely different story.

Assume that a colleague of yours (at your work place) always calls you 'fat.' He says so jokingly, so you do not pay much attention to him. You do not want to convey that you are more sensitive than you ought to be. But when he addresses with this word time and again, you decide you would stop him from telling you that you are fat.

Hence, you say, "I do not like it when you call me fat. I want that should stop saying this to me." These words are good. You think that you have done the right thing. But the problem is that when you were telling this to him, you had a smile on your face. The meaning of smile is that you are serious about whatever you are stating. You are inadvertently behaving in a particular way. But the opposite meaning is taken from the behaviour.

When serious words are said with a smile, the person in front of us gets a mixed message. The other person cannot take your request in a serious manner in such a situation. In comparison with the basic attack, this situation can be one that can make you feel dejected. You muster enough courage and tell someone hat he should not cal you 'fat' and he does not bother about your request. Whatever you say with a smiling face, eventually leads to the conclusion, "All right! If you call me 'fat', I would not mind it."

But someone bothers you even after that, you would state that it does not matter much if you tell others what's in your mind. That's because they do not take you seriously, so they act in this manner.

You cannot bring change in your behaviour in a Jiffy. We are not telling you to do this either. You have to increase your awareness through these practice exercises. You must understand that you clearly state a thing many times and its mutually conflicting meaning can be understood (by others).

Conflict or Flight?

As has already been told, your feelings produce reactions of various kinds in your body. You may be happy sad, terrorized, angry etc.—in every situation, your body reacts, especially during tense circumstances (in that case, the posture of "conflict or flight" is produced in your body so that you may be able to make yourself ready for your defense).

On an occasion, you make up your mind to have a face-off. You can take a decision to raise your voice in your support. Then, you repeat what's in your mind. Whatever you think, you tell the other person. Then, hormonal secretions increase in your body. Your heart beat increases. Your breathing rate may also soar. All these are the symptoms that indicate that you are ready for the fight.

Many incidents of this type can occur in your life. Then, you do not worry about the result, nor do you think that you may feel dejected due to its effect. Many people acquire the posture of conflict when they see that their child is facing a danger. Some people see that injustice is being done, so they come in the posture of fighting. In such conditions, you get help when your body prepares itself for the battle. That's because the spirit of setting things right is much more effective than the fear present in your mind, howsoever noble person you may be.

You have the following alternatives on some occasions—flight, i.e., you move back, forgive the rival or postpone the conflict. You move away from the circumstance. Many conditions arise when you sacrifice your desires and needs for the sake of others.

The flight of this type means that you are still living in a sea of hardships and that you are not going to escape them. 'Flight' can also mean that you want to get out of a relationship. It can also mean that you are leaving a job. I can also mean the ending of a friendship. While doing all this, you do not let your emotional experiences be disclosed to other persons.

6

Live Life at Your Own Will

We have already discussed that we become too much noble because of our own liking, although we do not feel that we are becoming so. If you select a behaviour of this type, you also have the ability to get rid of it. You can start with the selection of other alternatives.

Practice Is a Must

In this book, some effective alternatives have been discussed. We have also described in this text how you can use such alternatives in an effective manner. We are not trying to tell you that you bring about change overnight by following a few formulae. Change is not possible at such high speeds.

The art of saying 'No' is not an art that you can learn by reading a course book.

It is an art that needs practice. You make mistakes and then, you rectify yourself. That way, this art is developed and with passage of time, it becomes part of your habit.

There is no fixed way but there are many ways available for this. It is also possible that minor alterations may be done in your preset behaviour to make it useful for you. As soon as you bring one or two changes in your behaviour, you would be amazed to see the effect (of your behaviour on others).

In order to continue the effort of this type, it is important that you consider life as a game.

Being too much noble (beyond one's capacity) not an

ordinary thing. When you face crisis, shame or anger, it can prove to be highly lethal. We are not discussing those results that you are afraid of and due to which you have to face difficulties. The life story of such persons makes you sad. They have to face bitterness in life, for they are trying to develop coordination and when they fail, they leave themselves to be punished.

But since this is a serious type of behaviour, its results are also serious. We are not able to see all facts and a prosperous life continues to thrive around us.

Through it, we do not want to tell you that you accept the thing that you do not feel, or you laugh it, away, or you tolerate the bad behaviour of others, for you have been doing so for a long period. But if you follow the alternatives appended in this book, you would develop a sense of humour inside you. You would start enjoying some things.

We know that changing behaviour is one of the most difficult tasks. That's because the roots of problems lie in your childhood. So, a particular behaviour is connected with you for a long duration (starting somewhere in the past). Whatever effort would be made to change it, you would certainly try to oppose it. What's more, other people, who are part of your life, would also oppose it. Your family members and friends also like an excessively noble person, just like you, for their own life becomes easy that way.

Probably, if you face opposition from all sides, you can see that you have to face opposition from your own self as well. Your own inconvenient and agonizing emotional experiences are opposing you. There are many sad memories inside your body. Probably, you would know what to do and understand why that very method can be the best one. But your body would react upon seeing change. There would be cramps in stomach. Your throat would become dry. The breathing rate would also increase.

Many times, the dilemmas that surround us ought to be looked at in a logical manner. If we do so, it becomes difficult for us to believe them. We aver, "Why did I get into an imbroglio of this type?" When we see the light side of a crisis, it becomes easy for us to muster strength and maintain control (which we had inadvertently handed over to others earlier). Then, you have an opportunity to do something and change the situation.

For the sake of bringing about change, some practice exercises, reactions and thoughts have been presented like games. You would certainly like to implement or follow these exercises but you would be the only player in these games. It is an interesting facet. No one would know that you have already started the process of change in your inside. People can get a different result while dealing with you. It can be different from the result they had been hitherto accustomed to.

But when you are the only player of a game, you would have enough power and you would also relish going through the entire process.

Looking at these scenarios in the background of game has only one objective—when you apply them in your real life, the contradictory situation (of your real life) would not be able to affect you.

We also know that the more interesting we make the process of change, the easier it would be for us to get involved in that process. We hope that you would try to complete this seemingly impossible task by enjoying it at every moment. We want you to accept the challenges of change. You should not feel that you alone are trying to climb Mount Everest without the help of any guide. In the beginning, learn to climb small hills. Leave Everest for experienced climbers.

In this book, small wins have been discussed. We invariably experiment to get small victories. When you try to change everything in just one go while facing a situation, there are more chances of getting failure as a result. We are not stating that you do not try. But you start with a small beginning. While doing something new, take smalls steps.

When you would start tasting small victories—and that is easy too—you would start feeling that you have also become capable of solving big issues. You would have sufficient experience and due to it your self-confidence would become stronger by the day. It is not easy to practice with such issues due to which you are agonized first and repentant later. It would not be an easy effort and it is also possible that you may decide to stop the efforts mid-way.

In this book, the experiences of some people have been appended. Had these people selected another development, they would have faced different results. These are the circumstances which had transpired in the life of people. Since they were highly noble, they had to face inconvenience, despondency and lassitude. Besides they also had to face the agony of losing their identity.

When you put yourself in similar situations and think (just like we know that some scenarios are quite familiar), it would be necessary to remember that you have more than one alternative. We have also discussed some methods upon reading which you can say, "I can never do this." Or, there can be other method which, when read by you, would force you to state, "Yes, I would like to try this."

A Note on Families

In this book, some incidents and situations have been discussed that people face every day. Some of those incidents and situations present more difficult challenges than others.

There is a field in which we face more difficulties on the behavioural front. That field is—family. Your family would present unique problems before you. Still, it is important for you to keep a tab on the following during the course of discussion on events and solutions.

1. Every family is unique. You understand this point on the basis of your logic. But when you plan to change your behaviour with your family members, a particular technique is not of use to you. You tolerate behavioural patterns of your family members that you would never tolerate if they are displayed by your colleagues or friends.
2. In most families, there is a fixed way of dialogue. In most cases, it is decided even before the birth of a child. It also continues in the future. It seems that it would remain. Just like you learnt how to walk and talk, you would also have learnt how to establish dialogue in a natural manner. You would not have any other alternative.
3. "I only want to understand them." There would be many situations in which a unique (original) behaviour would be needed to change an old method. Some other situations would demand love and soft behaviour from your side.

7

Get Rid of Bondage

It seems to be very weird when the question of changing your behaviour crops up and your language is mentioned at the very first instance. When you want to change your adopted and learnt behaviour, it may be seem very weird to discuss your language. But this is not that weird.

Think about it for one moment. You go towards your old memories. Remember the things, said earlier, from this book; these should be those things that had affected your mind. Many of you must have tolerated cruelty and those must have been your most touching experiences. But language makes such an environment that you are forced to change your natural behaviour.

Parents use many methods to control the behaviour of children. Some effective methods are – laughing at children, insulting them, making them feel lowly, ignoring what they want or feel and other such methods. They are forced to think according to the directives of their parents. This can be done with the help of language alone, with resorting to physical violence.

Besides, many from among you must be having school experiences. For example, you may have been badly insulted by your teacher in the presence of your classmates. The teacher must have done because you had given a wrong answer, taken a nap in the classroom, got poor marks or come late to the classroom. When you are laughed at in full public view, it is ensured that such an incident would not be repeated. Thus, you would do anything so that the incident is not repeated. You would not like to face similar shame and insult yet again.

Many from among you must have been witnesses to that incident (when someone else was mocked at) and you must have been told that you yourself must also keep away from such habits. As soon as the scene of getting insulted crops up in your mind, you avoid doing that act again.

Your thoughts are made with words. You see this word through your thoughts.

Is Your Language Very Sweet?

Language plays the most important role in giving shape to behaviour. What you want was expressed with the help of words. The words were used to reprimand, assure, give reward, threaten, persuade and incite. Words can be like slaps put across one's cheeks. They hurt our self-confidence and self-pride.

Language gets assimilated in our subconscious mind. We are unable to understand the meanings of words in our early days. Since those days, we listen to the words. Words are uttered by those people from who we are afraid or those who rule over us. And when we are not able to develop the capacity to raise our doubt about them, we continue to consider that their words are truth.

Some agonizing and hurting words were said to you. They got entrenched in your inside. Even today, when you know how to doubt others, you are hesitant, insofar as doubting about those words is concerned. You may find it difficult to cast doubt over the statement of your mother which she could have said in sheer desperation. She could have said, "Expecting anything from you is useless. Why am I expecting anything from you?"

Language—the words told to you—influences you

deeply. That's why when we talk of changing our behaviour, we want to ponder over words first.

First of all, we start with a simple sentence. People use it to say sorry. They say, "I am sorry."

In your daily life, this sentence is uttered by you many times.

People say sorry only when they feel that they have made a mistake. Besides, when someone imposes mistakes on them, they say sorry. When they feel that their behaviour was not right, they apologize. They also apologize for the behaviour of others. They say sorry when they see that the other person is dejected beyond compare. They ask for forgiveness even there is no valid reason for doing so.

The use of language becomes a habit for us. Similarly, the thinking behind which there is no taste or interest becomes our habit. The effect of language is so deep that most of the times, we are unable to understand what words we are using.

Due to the use of language, the size of our notions and self-realization is decided. They also become strong (due to language).

We can communicate our message to other people through the language of our body. We can also put across messages to others by uttering words. With the help of the language you use, you are, in fact, revealing your personality.

Your language sends strong signals. Due to those signals, other people learn how much straight and noble you are. If you continue to say sorry, or if you continue to use unclear words, people would take you in the wrong perspective. They would ignore you and make wrong opinions about you. You give them such means as can be used by them to bother you. They can also get the job (of their choice) done from you through such means.

The language of forgiveness and (seeking) permission is a type of invitation. It shows the dilemma that you want to say something but something else is uttered by your mouth. It seems that your real, basic statement is not able to come forward. So, no one is able to learn about your objective.

Some words and statements have been given ahead. You use them to communicate your massages to others. We shall look at them in a multi-level perspective, viz., superficial, daily talk, proverbs ad idioms. All of them are lessons. We start with a simple example.

The answering machine is an important device of the Twentieth century. One, who has this machine, tells others (through one's machine), "I am sorry. I am not available to talk to you...." Why does the machine apologize? Why doesn't it say, without asking for an apology, "Please record your message. I shall try to contact you at the earliest possible moment?"

The makers of such types of machine had proposed the logic that they use a language in this machine that is in vogue in society.

This machine is also an example of how we believe in anything with our eyes closed. How much accustomed we are to behave in a particular manner that is expected from us. When someone wants to talk to you and you are not available, it is expected that you would say worry to that person. You are also expected to talk to people at your earliest since people want to talk to you.

Language tells about you in different ways. If you are one among those people who always say sorry, your answering machine would also be like you and you would have to make small change in it. When you learn to control the "sorry words" coming out of your mouth, you would also change the opinion about your own self. You would also change your opinion about the way people react towards you.

If your machine tells the world that you are sorry because you are not available for chat (and promise that you would talk to the caller on a priority basis upon your return), you can change the message of the machine and thus give a message regarding change in your behaviour. Then, your machine would start saying to people, "I shall contact you when the need to do so arises."

Language of Sorry

First of all, talk about those words that come out of your mouth automatically in your daily life. Besides, let's discuss those sermons, pieces of advice and saying that you must have heard in your childhood years and that must have been the basic rules of the behaviour that was expected from you.

Use of Language in Daily Life

How do you say sorry? Whenever you tell someone to do something (and know that he does not want to do it), what do you say? When you tell a bad news to someone, what do you say? When you want to tell about a new thought, what words do you use?

Some similar words have been given ahead with the help of which you want to hide yourself and show your second-grade position. These are the words which tell others that you do not take yourself seriously. These words tell that there is no importance of your desires, thoughts, thinking and emotional experiences. That way, you tell about your weakness to people (who think that you are a stupid, lousy and useless person).

If you expect assurance, you use a language of this type.

These are like comments passed on our own selves which represent the feeling of inferiority.

Ponder over the following words:

- I am sorry.
- I am really very sorry.
- Did you mind?
- Is it possible if.....Yes!
- But!
- Yes, but.....
- Sure.
- That's sad.
- Excuse me.
- Would it be fine if I....?
- Would you mind if I.....?
- I do not believe that you would like it.
- Would you do me a favour?
- I do not want to over emphasize.
- Would you think about it?
- Probably, it would be unpleasant to hear.
- I am perfectly fine.
- This is not a big problem.
- Do you think that you would be able to do it?
- Please forgive for interfering.
- If I interfere, would you mind it?
- You would not like it.
- I can't do this.
- Leave it to me. I shall see.
- I won't mind.
- It's absolutely correct.

- Would it be fine for you?
- Don't ask me, I do not know.
- Please forgive me for bothering you.
- Please excuse me for giving you trouble.
- I want to feel sorry…
- I am sorry to bother you but….
- I shall do as per your wish.
- I do not mind.
- I don't know.
- I know that you know better but ...
- There was nothing I could do there.
- Are you very much angry with me?
- I feel ashamed even as I ask you but….
- I am not able to clarify my point.
- I feel I could not tell you clearly what I wanted to.
- I am of no use.
- Are you sure?
- I don't want to bother you.
- If I ask you a question, would you mind?
- All this is my mistake.
- All this has happened due to me.
- Do you need anything else from me?
- Can I do anything else for you?
- If you don't want, you can refuse….
- Please, don't be angry.
- I did not want to behave in a harsh manner.
- I expected this.
- I was expecting this.
- If you believe, it's OK.

- If you think it is right, it is fine with me....
- I really want to ask you something.
- Should we do?
- Can I interrupt you?
- I am really feeling bad but....
- No one listens to me.
- Everything is fine.
- I am sure you want this only.
- Do not put allegation on me.
- I am of no use...
- Whenever you think it fine, would you....?
- Do you think that it would be possible for you?
- Can you do me a favour?
- Till the time you do not have any objection.
- There is no value of my advice.
- I shall do it for you.
- Excuse me, can I interrupt you?
- Please forgive me for interrupting.
- If someone won't do, I shall.
- I want to state with complete honour.....
- When would you have time....

You can be alert towards the words being uttered by your mouth and add new words to the aforementioned list.

None of these is wrong. But when they are used time and again, or when they are used without carefully pondering over them, or when they are used to justify our behaviour, or when they are used to give alibis, or when they are used to give alibis, or when they are used to escape straight and direct statements, then problems are created.

These are simple words. The issue here is—how and why do you use them?

When you say sorry, you should by clear why you are saying so. Are you saying sorry for such a task (done by you), or are you asking for forgiveness because of your (poor) behaviour? If you are saying sorry for a wrong task done, go ahead. But if you are saying sorry because of your existence, such a type of apology would show your weak self-confidence.

Excessively noble people need the "sorry language" and permission from others due to practice. Our aim is to change the practice. We do not want to snatch your decent language due o which social interactions are possible. All of us must understand etiquette but we do not need the etiquette that harms us. Nor can we include alibi making and saying sorry (many times) in the category of etiquette.

When we say sorry for more number of times than needed, we see many hilarious episodes. You must have felt that many times. When 'sorry' is thrown on a person many times, that person also starts apologising.

Read the following example.

You: I am sorry. Really, I am very, very sorry.

He: No, no! It's alright. I won't mind it, really.

You: No, no! I am really ashamed. You would never forgive me.

He: There is an issue like forgiving.

I am sorry. You were very much bothered.

You: I leave it to you.

He: Please don't be sad. It is alright. I was hurt more than you.

So, this discussion does not come to an end.

Rules Related to Behaviour

Every family has its own rules. In every family, one single person rules. Alternatively, many persons rule. These persons decide how every member of their family should behave. In your childhood, you must have listened to and imbibed such rules.

Some of these rules are as follows:

- If you do not have to say something worthwhile, keep your mouth shut.
- Do not make a noise.
- Good children don't like this.
- Children should not cry.
- Be a man.
- Men do not feel pain.
- Crying is a job of women.
- Do good to others.
- Do good and cast it in the river.
- Children should not make a noise.
- If you do not cry, I will give you something.
- This is not a big problem.
- Patience is test only at the time of crisis.
- I don't get what I want.
- I know what you are thinking.
- You should be grateful.
- You must obey all commands of elders.
- Guests are like Gods.
- Go to your room.
- Stay till your father does not come home.
- Had I been in your place, I would never have done it.

- Play peacefully.
- Man becomes great due to etiquette.
- Character is the key to success.
- Fate can be changed through the exertion by man.
- When I was of your age....
- In my era....
- Think about the hungry children of Africa.
- You are breaking the heart of your mother.
- Face it like a man.
- Do not give them a chance o raise doubt.
- If everything goes haywire, do not come running to me.
- Had everyone's desires been fulfilled, beggars would not be roaming on roads.
- Man's needs can be satiated, not desires.
- You would have to share it.
- I can't even imagine that... What he would have said, had he been alive today.
- It's good that.....he left this world before seeing this day.
- I can't understand why we agree with every talk of children.
- You should be grateful.
- You are a person who forgets favours done to him.
- At last, you....
- You don't know what this is...
- Do not spill milk
- Do not break the plate.
- I don't love you anymore.
- Why can't be more....?

- Avoid being sentimental.
- You don't need this.
- How can you be so selfish?
- Don't tell your father.
- We do not discuss these things in our family.
- The meaning of family is—accountability.
- Be happy.
- You would be punished if you do not obey.
- You are just like your father/mother/grandfather/grandmother.
- Do not deform your face.
- We must always help others.
- When you would have children of your own, you would understand.
- The family was disgraced due to your deed.
- Because of you, the family had to feel ashamed.
- You are a weird child.
- We shall see.
- We shall see later.
- You are absolutely alright.
- You disappointed us.
- Commit my point to your memory.
- Your future is dark.
- If you do not rectify yourself, we shall send you to hostel.
- If you do not obey us, we shall not let you study further.
- We shall get you married off and then, we shall send you to your in-laws.
- What would neighbours think?

- Now, I can't listen to your loose talk.
- Can't you stop thinking about your own self only once?
- If you do not rectify yourself, I shall go away from you.
- Can you do this to us?
- We did not expect this from you.
- You have broken our heart.
- Talk according to your age.
- You never had a brain.
- Other members of the family are wise than you.
- More work, less talk.
- You cannot go out of home in this manner.
- I have not reared children so that they would behave with me in this manner.
- Who do you think you are?
- Do you want your head to be broken?
- Would you not stop doing mischief?
- You would understand when you grow up.
- Did I get this in lieu of what I did?
- There is no need to be afraid.
- You would take my life one day.
- Be calm. Why are you getting so much excited?
- I am ashamed of you.
- I would never be able to raise your head because of you.
- Do children suck the blood of parents only?
- Grow up, for God's sake!
- Till what time would you remain immature.

- When would you gain wit?
- There is no need to do any hypocritical act.
- Whatever you sow, so shall you reap.
- Who do you think you are?

Many parents would look at this list. Then, they would say, "Oh God! I did say such things to my children." You know that you say many things to your children. It's easy to say such things; they automatically come out of our mouth. Such things come out of your subconscious mind, they were told to you sometime in your childhood years. Children are told to shun such things (through these phrases) as are not liked by their parents. Thus, the will of elders is imposed on children; at least, efforts are done to do so.

Many other things must be cropping up in your mind; the same can be added to the list. With the help of them, you can also understand the rules that were in vogue in the era of your grandparents who believed in traditional thoughts. We are trying to carry on those beliefs, from one generation to the next one.

In this list, the area of religion has been excluded. When you are brought up, you are given moral education of various types on the basis of religion.

You are shown a way of living through your religion. You can also include religious sermons in this list. The notions related to religion, stories associated with it and lessons or principles connected with it can be included in this list, about these, you were probably briefed in your childhood years.

Did you ever have to face conflict in family due to its rules? Or, did your parents ever tell you that rules were being opposed (by you)? In such a case, the truth of acceptable and expected behaviour of a person can be different from the truth of another person. Then, who would be termed right?

This is like looking at the world through the eyes of a noble person. In this, your rules would become part of your opinion system. If there are two mutually conflicting systems under one roof, you would find that language is fighting. This situation of children can be full of dilemma.

Natural Qualities and Language

After seeing the aforementioned lists and adding some items from your own side (to these lists), you must become clear language has played a very important role in giving shape to your life. Words can hurt your self-confidence and make it week. The pinching, pricking and bitter things told to you led to the dilution of your self-confidence.

Such a language, if used this way, kills your natural virtues. The words told to you time and again became rules for you. It became necessary for you to live life on the basis of those rules. Since you absorbed those words in the beginning, your brain also has a rule book which tells what you should or should not do. Due to this, your natural virtues do not get a chance to develop.

The lack of natural qualities means that every event has been discussed, every worry has been removed and every possibility has been analyzed. You worry about the result of every task. You ask yourself, "What would happen if..."

"What would happen if....." A large portion of brain is occupied by this phrase; time and energy are also used up (in brain). Pondering over every possible result and thinking over every crisis is a painful process that makes you tired. When you are worried about what's going to happen, you do not take care about what's happening in the present. (This method may be effective in your childhood days but when you become an adult, it's of no use).

When you keep your eyes away from your present, it means that you are ignoring the crisis. If you do not live in your present and live in your imaginary world, you would go far away from your natural qualities. In that case, you would continue to follow predefined rules.

All these rules make you restricted; they put restrictions on you. They imprison you in a small and very narrow circle and so you are not able to cross the threshold of acceptable and good behaviour. These rules were prepared when you were little; you haven't forgotten them till date. They remain in your brain and guide you in whatever actions you take.

Imagine that you are taking part in a meeting. One part of you participates in the proceedings of the meeting. The brain tells you, "For me, I would be appropriate to keep quiet and sit here. My thoughts are of no use. I do not want to be a fool in front of others. God knows what all people (present in the meeting) would think about me. I am sure that those people do not give me importance. Hence, it would not be correct on my part to speak." Other similar negative thoughts.....

Dialogue continues in the brain of every person, it's impossible that this would not happen. But excessively noble people are always busy in conducting an internal dialogue related to doubt. When had you praised yourself last time (When you had done a good task)? Probably, you had not done so, or you had not done so properly, or someone else had praised you.

Small Things are Important

You should focus on your language, for the art of saying 'No' is deeply connected with language. Hence, there is a need to start in this direction.

First of all, focus on your internal language. The endless dialogue going on in your brain can be the easiest field for you. It would be a situation in which you would know that you are effecting change of some time and you won't have to speak with force for this.

Next time, when you listen to the voice of your brain, thank it and give a suggestion that it should praise you on some occasions (instead of censuring you at all times).

The next step would be to pay attention to the words being uttered by your mouth. Do not change. Just focus on them (to begin with). In the beginning, it would not be possible to change them. But if you remain alert towards your words, you would use new words while talking. Thus, you would be able to get rid of your old habit.

●

8

Five Methods of Saying 'No' with Decency

People always tell you to do something. Life is like that only. People mostly tell us to make such types of commitment—as are inconvenient for us. We do not have time for those commitments, or they are the ones that we do not want to do from the core of our heart. But, we are hesitant to say 'No.' So, we get prepared for the talk which we do not like.

You should develop the habit of saying 'No.' You would have to understand that if you say 'yes' to a thing or talk that you do not like, your life would be adversely affected. If you say 'yes' to everyone, you would be surrounded by unwanted tasks and this, you would not be able to do any task in a satisfactory manner.

First of all, you would have to learn which tasks should be given a nod (yes) by you and which ones should be shunned (refused for execution). You can take these decisions depending upon the realities of your life. You would have to decide which things are vital in your life. So, on the basis of positive thinking, you have to decide the goals of your life. Whenever you are told to do a task, ponder over that task by keeping your goals in full view. You decide whether by doing such a kind of task, you would be able to go near your goals or away from them. When you arrive at a conclusion that it would be apt for you to say 'No,' there are many decent ways of saying this. You can follow them and avoid hurting the feelings of others. You yourself would also escape the feeling of guilt that way. Try to be honest while saying 'No.' If you do so, you would not have any feeling of repentance in your mind.

Five Methods of Saying 'No' with Decency

There are five methods saying 'no' decently. They are as follows:

1. Say No Directly

Sometimes, it is better to say 'no' decently yet directly. If someone is telling you to do a task that he himself can do, it would be apt to say 'no' to him in a direct way. Similarly, those people, who generally tell you to do one task or the other, ought to be told, "I know that you yourself can do this task in a much better way than me."

2. Mention Your Busy Schedules

"As of now, I am busy doing other tasks," you can state. When you are busy, clearly tell people about your busy schedules. When you say so, people would understand that you do not have time. So, they would do something else to get their tasks done. You should never leave an ongoing task in the middle to do a totally new task.

3. Tell about Your Difficulty"

Currently, I am giving attention to my family/ career/personal life," you can state. If you have been going through a difficult patch of your life, do not accept any additional task upon the request of somebody. It is not necessary for you to describe the woes of your personal life. Just give a hint to the other person.

4. Tell Them You are Incapable

"I don't think that I am capable enough to do this task," you can state. If you feel that the task you are being told to do cannot be done by a man of your caliber, say 'no.' Express your helplessness and tell the other person that it is an important task. Tell him that if you did it, wrong result would come. No one would like to get any task done from you for getting bad result.

5. Give Alternatives

"I can't do it but I know a person who can do it," you may state. Use this method of saying 'no' when you know that another person can do the task in question. That person should also have enough time to do the task. Say 'no' and give an alternative, this would be a better option for you. But be careful—the person, whose name you are suggesting as an alternative, should agree to do the task. If he doesn't agree, it would be understood that you had tried to put off the task that was offered to you.

9

The Power to Say 'No'

'No' is a simple word. But for most of us, it is difficult to pronounce. Most people are heard saying, "I would be pleased" or "When do you need me?"

When children are two years of age, they say 'No.' At that time, their parent rule over them. Parents like to listen to 'No' from the mouth of their children.

When we grow up, we are told to keep everyone happy. The word 'No' is shunted out of our dictionary. We devise many ways to please people. We are not expected to say 'no' to powerful people and elders. But we know (in our heart) that we can escape many difficulties of life by saying 'no.'

- **Weak 'No'**

  There are many alibis or logical statements along with weak 'no'. When you are sans self-confidence, you start making alibis to support your 'no' so that the other person may be able to believe your *In such a situation, you are even ready to say sorry to say 'no.' This type of 'no' can have an adverse effect. Thus, a message can come out that you are using false alibis to avoid doing the task in question.

- **Effective 'No'**

  This is stated in an offensive manner. "Are you joking?" You can ask and then, you can add, "When you go out of town, I would do this task."

  Sometimes, through an effective 'no', the person

making a request is attacked. "It seems your brain has stopped working. I cannot do a task which is not important for me."

- **Powerful 'No'**

It is simple and straight. "No, I can't do it." If you have to tell the reason, say it in a few words. "No, I won't be able to do it. I am busy in some other task at present."

Methods of Making Powerful 'No' Easy and Simple

1. **If someone tells you to do a piece of work**, it would be appropriate to take time to ponder over it. When you consider the task, always keep in mind that the decision depends upon you.
2. **Use your body language to say powerful 'no'**. Take care—your voice should be powerful and clear. While saying 'no', look into the eyes of the other person and say 'no' while shaking your heed.
3. **Remember—saying 'no' is a respectable answer.** When you feel that it would be appropriate to say 'no' for something, say 'no' with honesty.
4. **When you want to say 'no,' your mouth utters 'yes.'** That way, you can feel restlessness. That way, your energy can be destroyed. You may have to face other problems as well. By saying 'no,' you can protect yourself from such problems.
5. **If you are saying 'no' to a person and you could** have helped him some other situation, clearly explain your busy schedules.

10

Saying 'No' is a Great Art

All people know that if you try to fulfill many promises at one point of time, you would not be able to remain productive. Your complications would keep on growing (in terms of number). You would not be able to do any task on time or nicely.

You are always requested and told to give your time. People contact you over telephone, e-mail or at a personal level. In order to remain productive and escape stress, you would have to learn the art of saying 'no'. It is an art which most people are reluctant to learn.

Why is saying 'no' deemed to be such a difficult task? In fact, you feel that if you say 'no' to someone, he would feel hurt in emotional terms. He can be angry with you, or he can be full of languor. So, it is not easy to say 'no.' Secondly, when you feel that you may need a particular person in the future too, you want to maintain cordial relationships with him. So, you do not want to spoil your relationship with him by saying 'no.'

If effort is made, the art of saying 'No' can be learnt. Some such methods have been discussed ahead, as follows:

1. Understand the Value of Your Time

Understand your commitments and understand the value of your time. In that situation, if a person demands your time for a new task, you can decide that it would not be possible for you to do that task. You can say to him, "I can't do it now. I have many other tasks to do."

2. Understand Your Priorities

Assume that you have some spare time. Nowadays, people rarely have spare time. Even then, you ask yourself a question—should the new task that you are going to take up necessarily consume your spare time? If you remain busy in pleasing people, you would be left with no or little time for your family. Spending time with wife and children can be more important than satisfying others.

3. Practise to Say 'No'

The practice of saying 'no' can lead us to this habit. In our daily life, if we practice to say 'no,' we can develop it as a habit. Sometimes, we can repeat this word in front of a stubborn person and thus escape being pressurized. Whenever someone tries to pressurize you, you should easily refuse. That way, you can protect yourself from people.

4. Do Not Apologize

Some people say, "I am sorry but..." after saying 'no.' They think that it is a decent act. Although decency is important, your side becomes weak if you apologize. While saving your time, you should be clear and avoid any kind of apology.

5. Stop Becoming a Good Man

If you try to be a fine man on the insistence of one and all, you may be in trouble. If people feel that your time or money can be easily used, they would continue to misuse this weakness of yours. But if you raise a wall around yourself, people would start looking for other weak people. You tell people that you alone own your time. So, say 'no' to all those things that are not part of your priorities.

6. Don't Tell Boss

Mostly, we feel that we should say 'yes' on every talk of our boss, for it is our helplessness. We feel that if we say 'no,' our weakness would be revealed to boss. But you can say 'no' to your boss as well. You can tell him that if you take up many responsibilities at one time, your productivity can be affected. You are unable to take care of the existing responsibilities either. If your boss imposes new responsibilities on you, tell him to decide the priority of all tasks once again. That's because you can do only one task at a time.

●

11

Types of Limits to be Decided to Say 'No'

In our daily life, we have to face many types of request of others. Helping others is a good habit but if we do this regularly, we are not left with enough time to satisfy our own needs. If we do not have energy, time and desire to do some tasks, lassitude starts developing in our inside if we are given those tasks (to please others).

Whenever someone requests us to do any task, the feeling of saying 'no' is generated in our inside but we are unable to say 'no' due to the lack of self-confidence. Why does this happen? There are some reasons behind this, as follows:

- You are afraid that people would dislike you, or you have a feeling of keeping everyone satisfied.
- You always want to keep yourself busy so that you may be able to preset yourself as a busy and important person.
- You feel that there is no importance of spare time and it is better to be busy in the tasks of others instead of sitting without work.
- You are perplexed by the result of saying 'No.' Due to that result, you are unable to say 'No.'

When you define limits and learn to say 'No,' your life starts improving. For this purpose, you need to speak clearly and you also have to tell your objective in a lucid manner. The decision to refuse the request of your kin, friends and colleagues is your personal decision.

At work place, in your family and among your friends, you can use wisdom and skill. Thus, you can learn to say 'no' with dignity (in all these groups). A few formulae have been appended ahead. You can adopt them and learn the art of saying 'No.' They are as follows:

1. **Ensure that you know all facts:** Before making any promise, ensure that the task that you are being requested to do is well known to you. If there are no complete sets of information regarding that task, you can be mistaken. Thus, you may face trouble while taking decisions. You have the right to ask the other person about the task.
2. **Ask yourself—is this an unreasonable request?:** Whenever a person requests, he has an axe to grind (in the task). The person who is approached through this request is not focused on and his interests are ignored. When the request is heard and you feel that it is not appropriate and inconvenient to you, say 'no' directly. Whenever you develop the feeling of listening to a request and also, feel a sense of hesitation inside you (after listening to that request), it would not be right to say 'Yes' in that condition.
3. **Take Time:** There is no rule that someone makes a request to you and you have to answer promptly. Take time before taking a final decision and thus ponder over the issue. You can say, "I need some time to think about it. I shall think and tell you."
4. **Decide the goal:** When you finalize a goal it becomes easy for you to say 'no.' When you decide your priorities, it becomes easy to decide how much time you can spend for others without hurting your own interests. Then, it would be easy for you to reject those requests that are against your priorities.

5. **Speak clearly, without any alibi or apology:** When you know all facts and have decided to say 'no,' say 'no' in a peaceful yet lucid manner. You can use high-pitch voice, appropriate physical posture and right style of eyes to tell the person that you are firm on your decision.

   Do not be weak. Say 'no' without hesitation. If you hesitate, it would appear as if you yourself are in a fix over the decision. If you say, "I am sorry but...," your side would be considered to be weak.

6. **Do not be afraid of pressure:** If you feel that the other person can pressurize you to get something accepted by you, do not be nervous. Repeat your decision in your mind. Clearly present your view in front of the other person. Do not change your decision under any kind of pressure. No means no. you have the right to stick to your decision.

7. **Consider the decision to say 'No' to be in your favour:** Consider the decision to say 'no' as the one that is for your welfare. You have used your perseverance to decide to say 'no' and this decision is in your favour.

12

It's Not Difficult to Say 'No'

Are you burdened by work, or are you full of tension? In the busy era of today, you are not the only person of this type. If you want to avoid stress and control your time, you would have to develop the habit of saying 'no' to every new task. Many times, you want to say 'no' but due to hesitation, you say 'yes.' So, you are troubled by additional work burden later. If you learn to say 'no,' you do welfare of your own self and your kin. So, tension level can be reduced that way and time can be used to do important tasks.

How to Say 'No'

1. Just say, "I can't do it now." Use a voice that full of sympathy but with a serious tone. If you are asked the reason, say that you are busy in another task. Now, change the topic. Most wise people would be satisfied by this answer. But if a person pressurizes you again and again, repeat, "I am busy in another task." Then, change the topic. Move away from that place, if need be.
2. If you find it inconvenient to say 'no' clearly, or if the other person is very stubborn (and requests time and again), you can say, "I will think it over first. Then, I will tell you." When you say so, you get a chance to review your work plan. You can do costing analysis too. You can visualize the result of doing a new task and give your answer on the basis of these things. So, you can circumvent additional work load that way.

3. If you like the request of a person but do not have enough time to execute his task, you can say to him, "I cannot do this. But I can try to do this." Thus, you can make a commitment to do a small or unimportant part of the task. So, you would attach yourself to that task only partially but you would do this on your terms.

Important Tips

1. Do not try to be defensive, nor should you express sorry. Say 'no' in a clear and decent way. That way, the other person would get the message that you are a sympathizer but would not change your decision under pressure.
2. If you want to give answer to a person after wards, focus on facts and do not give answer in an assuring manncr (to the other person). If that person fees that your answer can be 'yes,' he would feel very sad and dejected when you would tell him 'no' later.
3. If you are told about the reason to say no, always remember that you are not bound to obey him. You can say, "It is not possible in my busy daily schedule."

Remember—work hours are limited. Accepting any new task means—the task at hand would be affected. If you take up a new task, you have to sacrifice your previously allotted time for taking rest and looking after your own self.

13

Say 'No' with Dignity

It is not easy to deny the request of a friend. But sometimes, it becomes necessary to say 'no' to him. When you are not in a position to accept the request, balance yourself and refuse without losing control over yourself. If you are not ready to say 'no', you would always utter 'yes.'

Necessary Steps

1. **Listen to request carefully:** When a person makes a request to you, do not interrupt him and listen to him carefully.
2. **Make your 'No' brief to the maximum possible extent**: Do not raise your voice. Do not get peeved either. Say directly that you cannot do the task at the present time. Whenever you say 'no', say it with self-confidence and in a controlled voice. That way, the other person would be affected by your answer.
3. **There is no need to give the reason in detail:** The reason is not to be described in deep detail. If a reason is asked from you, say, "I won't be able to do it." After this, stop discussing that topic.
4. **Tell about the reason behind your will with case:** If you feel that it is necessary to mention the reason behind your 'no,' try to tell in an easy, complacent manner.
5. **Stick to your decision:** If the person making a request is not ready to accept your 'no,' tell him, in clear words, that you are not going to change your decision in any case.

Useful Tips

1. Behave with utter decency, even if the person making a request is not decent.
2. If you say 'no' and someone else is bothered by your refusal, keep quiet; be peaceful. If need be, move away from the venue.
3. While giving the reason behind your refusal, do not tell lies.

Before saying 'No,' you should say, "What are you trying to say? I am unable to understand this." That way, the other person would not be disappointed.

●

14

How to Say 'No' Without the Feeling of Guilt

'No' is an ordinary word but sometimes, using it becomes very difficult. People use it while dealing with their life partner or children. But when the time comes to say 'no' to a person outside the family, the person feels hesitant.

It is important to decide when and how one should say 'no.' It does not mean that you should worry only about your interest and never help others. But the problem arises when you accept a thing and become tense, problems arise.

- **When you really want to do something, say 'Yes':** When you listen to a person's request and feel that the person's task ought to be done, or if you think that the task in question is appropriate for the goalsor success of your life, say 'yes' in such a situation.
- **It is not necessary for you to be busy to say 'No'**: If you plan to spend your evening in the company of family members and/or watch TV in the company of near and dear ones and are invited at that point of time, it does not mean that you should accept the invitation. Taking time out for our own self is as important as taking time out for others. Try o understand the value of your time. Remember one thing—When you say 'yes' for anything, you are, in fact, saying 'no' for some other thing. Whenever this happens, you may be ignoring important facets of your life, viz., family, career, spiritualism etc. For example, your child is told that you help his school's committee. You get involved

in the tasks of the committee and cannot give adequate time to your child. Similarly, by saying 'yes' to people seeking donation, you are, in fact, saying 'no' to your financial future.

- **Do not say 'Yes' immediately, take time for thinking:** Whenever you are requested to do a piece of work, look at the tasks at hand. Take a deep breath and think. Otherwise, you would continue to say 'yes' to every task that would come to you and your life would become difficult.
- **If you practise, it is easy to say 'No':** When you have to say 'No' to somebody for the first time, you face trouble. But when you feel that by saying 'no,' you have taken the right step, your self-confidence increases. This dexterity can be learnt through practice. The more you start experimenting, the easier it becomes for you to say no.
- **When you say 'Yes' and get restless from inside, it means that you should have said 'No':** When you say 'Yes' but did not want to do so, you develop a feeling of restlessness. The result of this feeling of restlessness can't be conducive to your interests.
- ***When you trust your capability, it is easy to say 'No':*** When you say 'No' too forcefully and do not apologise for this, your self-confidence oozes out. Thus, your determination towards your capabilities increases. Some people say 'No' and then, they start giving clarification. That way, the other person sees that they lack self-confidence (after saying 'no').
- **You do not have to be dry and ill-tempered:** There can be many methods of saying 'no.' For example, you can state, "I cannot help you now." You can say, "I can do this task next month." You may aver, "It is not possible for me." Or, you can say with case, "No, thank you."

15

Useful Formulae for Saying 'No'

In order to keep life comfortable and felicitous, it is very much important to know about the useful formulae for saying 'no.' These very formulae are being discussed in this chapter, as follows:

1. Say Briefly

Give your answer briefly and in a few words. Avoidgiving any clarification to support your reply.

2. Be Decent

While refusing the request of the other person, remain decent. You can say, "I am sorry I would not be able to attend dinner along with you tonight.
Thanks for inviting me."

3. Remain in Control

Be peaceful. Say 'no' in a straightforward manner. Remain sympathetic towards the person who has requested you.

4. Be Honest

In order to say no, you can honestly tell your side of the story and give logic. Be open in giving that reason to the other person. That way, an appropriate effect is felt by the other person.

5. Say 'No' and Move Ahead

Many times, the person making the request listens to your 'no' and even then, he tries to pressurize you. Due to this, a situation of delusion can be created. In such a case, it is better to say 'no' and move ahead.

6. Practise

Practise what you have to state. Practise in front of a mirror. While doing so, imagine about the situation in which you are supposed to say 'no' to someone.

Six Techniques of Saying 'No'

1. Straight forward 'No'

Under this technique the objective is to say 'no' without apologizing. If the other person has a problem, do not let him impose his problem on you. Straight forward 'no' is effective.

2. Uncertain 'No'

Under this technique, the request of the present is deferred, not negated (rejected). This is not a certain 'No' and both parties can talk about it in the future as well. If you feel that you can accept the request later, use this technique. For example, "I cannot send the letter tonight but can certainly do so in the morning tomorrow."

3. 'No' Said with Wisdom

Under this technique, we understand the spirit of the request and then, we say 'no.' In this method, the requested fully rejected. Thus, no scope is left for talk in the future. For example, "I know that this letter is important but I cannot go to the post office tonight."

4. Alternative 'No'

It is not certain and through it, the possibility of continuing the discussion remains intact. You can use this technique in such a condition in which you feel that you can do a piece of work but are uncertain about the issue of timing. For example, "Can I go at some other time for the sake of your work?"

5. 'No' With a Reason

Through this technique, the brief yet correct reason behind 'No' is given. When you do not want to make the other person full of agony (but have good reasons to reject his request), you should use this technique. For example, "I cannot go to send the letter tonight because I have to meet my friend."

●

16

Saying 'No' Can be Made Easy

If you remain highly alert towards your behaviour, emotional experiences, needs and desires, you would also be equally capable in changing them, even if the change may not be done in an exact manner. When you ponder over what you do and how you feel, you would start getting success. Then, you would not take the meaning of 'change' as 'success.

The meaning of remaining aware means that you should take care of the following aspects.

Emotional Experiences

When you face a situation which you think is out of your control, what kinds of feeling crop up in your mind? What other people want from you and how you satisfy your needs? When you face both these situations at the same time, what kinds of emotional experience are felt by you?

Physical Postures

What are your physical postures while talking to people about your own self? When you are giving your introduction with utter humility, what do you really do?

Language

When you are becoming excessively noble, what types of word do you utter?

Give Rest to Brain

Your brain works hard to serve your interests. On this basis, you treat a thought as true and follow it. In your personal life, many notions thrive. They may or may not be true. But you have the faith that they are true, so you decide the direction of your behaviour. The only way find out whether a notion is true or not is to ask.

If you do not have the information, it's just possible that the notion that you had made may be totally opposite to reality. You consider your notion to be correct and think in your favour, unlike others. This notion can be exactly the opposite as well.

Selection

Always remember this thing in your brain the right to like is always yours. There is also a time when you do not feel but when you have to take a decision, develop a habit of selecting from among alternatives. When you know that you have selected the best alternative, task remains under your control.

Life is a Game

The goal of increasing your awareness and changing your behaviour should be considered to be a game by you. That's because you are the only player in this game. So, no one else is in the game but you. You can take the game towards its culmination, or you can leave it midway, or you can refuse to play.

Small Victories

One cannot change one's own self overnight. Do not try to bring about change in one go. It would not be feasible to do so. Win small battles so that you may be able to build your self-confidence and enthusiasm.

Control Your Smile

When you smile, its direct meaning is understood as "you are not serious." Upon seeing this, any person can request you review it from the beginning. But you have already rejected the request. The other person sees the smile on your face and feels the softness that you have. It is important that the way you want others to take you seriously, you should also take yourself seriously.

Look into the Other Person's Eyes

For some people, it is very difficult to look into the eyes of others for a long period. When you do not look into eyes and looking sideways, it means you are not interested in the subject being discussed. If a person is not able to see your face clearly, he is not able to comprehend the seriousness of your words.

Stand at Your Place

When you slide backwards, there is no effect. This is considered to be a weakness. Then, the correct signal of your goal is not received. When you go backwards, the other person is not able to understand why you are doing so. So, they interfere in the empty space on their own will. When you stand at your place with firmness, your goal gets strength. This means that you should remain firm at your place in physical and vocal terms.

Put across Your Point Clearly

It is not necessary that you have to speek at a high pitch of voice to put your point across to the other person. Most people commit this very mistake. You do not have to make people feel what you want by raising your voice level. Rather, clearly state, in a powerful way, what the meaning of your speech really is.

Tell the Truth

That way, other persons can understand how you feel. That way you can convey that you are not very comfortable with what other people are doing or saying. It may be difficult to tell the truth, for you feel that it is not easy to reveal. But that is needed for defining the limit and resolving the conflict. That way the entire position is clarified.

Do Not Change Topic

You may be engaged in a discussion in which you would not like to take part. But you have to do it since the other person is inciting you to do so. In such a situation, the other person can change the topic and present such a logic through which he can pressurize you.

Agreement

If someone says to you, "You are talking like a fool," you agree with him. Then he cannot extend the discussion. "I think you are emotional. Is that true?" he can ask you. Thus, you reply, "Yes, you are right." When you say so, the other person gives up.

Do Not Accuse

If you want to tell someone that you do not like his behaviour, start with the sentences that describe how you feel. Do not mention his limitation. When you raise your accusative finger towards a person, he comes in a defensive mode and thus is no longer keen to listen to you.

Do Fixed Arguments

Ensure that the direction of discussion is previously decided. Keep away from useless talk. Avoid repeating old logical statements.

Make Bridges

Give the other person such a thing that he should also become willing to give you something in return. You can offer him a cup of tea or coffee. You can show sympathy for him. That way you can pull him towards your side.

Find Out Why You Don't Get What You Want

There can be many reasons behind this. Be cool-minded and try to find out. Why don't you get what you desire? That way, you can move ahead.

Change in Desire

When you find out why desired things do not come to you, it does not at all mean that you cannot acquire anything. You can change your desire and get the things of your liking from others. Thus, you can add small victories to your account.

Take Time

Creating a conducive environment for controlling your emotional experiences or despair is possible only when you do many small tasks. In order to keep away from any situation, keep a few alibis ready and understand well before arriving at a conclusion.

Slow Down Your Speed

In order to present your talk in an effective way, use smile and small sentences. If a person leaves gaps deliberately, in the hope that you would fill those gaps, control this tendency. Let the other person feel inconvenience for change.

Say 'No' with speed

In the very beginning of the discussion, aim at the right target. You can change your decision later. If you say 'no' quickly, the other person would be deeply affected. He would not be able to ignore your response.

Wait for One Minute

When you feel that whatever you have said or done just now, is not correct, you can state, "Please don't mind. Wait for one minute. No, I won't be able to do it." If you say so, you and the other person become alert that you want to stay and need some time.

You Can Change Thought

After learning the fact, you can change your thought even 2 minutes, 2 hours, 2 months or 2 years later. Although you would be reminded, time and again, about the assurance you had given. But when the time comes, you won't be able to do that, or you won't take interest.

Don't Give Clarification

Never apologise. Never give any clarification. Do not give full to the other person which he can use against you.

Talk Briefly

Expending talk is not good. If you do so, the other person gets a noose for you. You can be captured with the help of that noose. Whenever you want to say anything, be brief.

Keep Many Alternatives with You

Instead of saying directly, you can also say that since you cannot after any kind of help, you have a possible alternative in which you would not be involved. The more the number of the alternatives suggested by you, the lower pressure the other person would try to create on you.

Repeat Your View

Repeat your view so that that the other person should be able to correctly understand your intention. That way, you can remain firm on your stand. Also take care that your behaviour should not show any sign of peevishness.

Humour

Use humour to reduce tension and resolve a difficult situation. In order to ensure that you do not flow along with the viewpoint of the other person, use humour which is an effective way of protection.

Look from a Factual Viewpoint

Look at any problem, conflict or dispute from a factual angle. See the situation like a non biased, non-aligned observer and forget that your interest is attached to the outcome.

Ignore the Problem

An effective way of not associating with a problem can be—ignore the problem. Use it when the problem being presented is entirely of the person who has come to present it to you. He is expecting a solution from you, or he is trying to associate with yet another problem. In such a condition, you should dissociate yourself from the problem and let the person in question look for a solution on his own.

Standard Game

It reminds us of the quality that we associate with the behaviour of high or low level. When behaviour is changed on the plea of standard, thought is not given any priority. Remember that other people tell you about the concept of "standard game" to cut down stress level so that they may be able to impose their own will on you.

Ten Positive Facets of High-standard Behaviour

- Be superior to the other person in physical terms.
- Take your time.
- Use silence.

- Stand straight.
- Talk in a clear and controlled voice.
- Repeat your talk.
- Listen with passing any comment.
- Rise above discussion.
- Be firm on your place.
- Talk to the other person by looking into his eyes.
- Avoid being impressed by false logic.
- Do not apologize. Do not give any clarification.
- Define clear limits.

Positive Features of Low-level Behaviour

- Talking to the other person at the same (physical) level or by bending towards the other person.
- Talking in slow, sympathizing tone.
- Showing wisdom and leaning.
- Show sympathy towards the emotional experiences of the other person.
- Being sad or agonized according to the statements given by the other person.
- Looking at ground.
- Using the body language in a posture of sympathy.
- Apologizing again and giving justification.
- Showing the limit clearly.

Change in Situation

When there is a great space in the situation, you would find it very useful to follow these rules while talking to your parents or any other person.

- Do not try to express that the other person is in the wrong; nor should you try to make him believe that you are correct.

- Be patient to the maximum possible extent.
- Listen to the other person carefully and respect his emotional experiences.
- Avoid arguments.
- Do not give clarification on such topics that cannot be understood with such clarifications.
- Do not accuse that the other person is controlling your life, although you may be feeling that he is doing so.
- Do not extend argument.
- Stay firm on your point.

You Would Have to Change Yourself to Change Others

This book would help you bring about change in your own self. You would stop hoping that others would change your life and make your life easy. This means that you would have to control your own life.

From this book, you would get the inspiration that it is better to become a psychological capable or strong person instead of becoming a psychologically tortured person. So, become the builder of your own fate. After that, you would only have to practice regularly.

17

Do You Like to Avoid Conflict?

Those people, who are noble, do not like to indulge in conflict. How do you deal with conflict? Do you argue in an excited state, or do you adopt a peaceful method to express your disagreement? Are you one among those people who do not bother about their own agony but take more care so that the feelings of the other person are not hurt? Are you one of those persons who like to sit in a corner before the moment of conflict arrives?

When you are excessively noble, you would not like to indulge in arguments and discussion. If there is an environment of chaos around you, the lack of peace within you can be reflected. Hence, you would adopt a skill and show as if there were no type of chaos around you!

It is possible that you may become deaf only temporarily and feign that you are not listening to what others are saying. It's just possible that you may have developed the dexterity to keep yourself away from the chain of events. You can give an excuse that you have to attend an important meeting, or you have to catch a train. You can create many alibis of this type and run away from the battleground.

Are You in Favour of Maintaining Peace?

Can you play the role of Switzerland? It is a country that remains mental towards both the nations that are at war with each other. You can be a person who listens to the viewpoints of both sides but never supports one particular side. Or, you can be a person who never expresses his agreement or disagreement in an open manner.

It is also possible that you simplify a difficult or stressful situation so that you may not have to face a problem. You keep such things on a level and due to those things, it becomes difficult for you to move ahead.

Can you make yourself such an invisible or self-centred creature that can fade into the oblivion upon smelling a conflict? Or, you can adopt a neutral stance, which has been explained earlier, and ignore the danger. You can be reluctant to avoid the moment of truth. You can tell a lie so that you may be able to escape controversies.

If you dislike conflict to such an extent that you lay down your arms even upon smelling it, it is possible that you may be expressing some dissent. But you know that you would accept the will of others. You would give them what you want. You would let them have their own way. You would let them conclude that they are right and you are in the wrong.

When you disagree, you would express your consent. You would accept even the wrong arguments of others. You would accept even their wrong defence tactics. You would try to justify the wrong behaviour of another person so that you may not have to face the problem of getting hurt or troubled and that may start an argument. It's also possible that you may feel sorry upon seeing that others are troubled whereas you were not at all in the wrong in the issue in question.

Now, read the following example.

The other person can be your partner, colleague, friend, relative, life partner or anyone else. That does not make much difference. For practice, you can imagine about a person who gives you trouble and thus, you can imagine that you engaged in a conversation with him.

Second Person (SP): Would you do one task for me?

You: First of all, tell me what's to be done?

SP: A packet has come for me from outside. It is lying at Transport Nagar. You go by car and bring that packet to me.

You: But, I don't think that I would be able to bring it. I would have to remain busy throughout the day.

SP: How does that matter if you go for a while? See, I would do this throughout the day. Someone has to bring it.

You: Right. But it wouldn't be easy for me to bring it. I won't go towards that side. I don't think I would be able to do it.

SP: Leave it. This is not a tough task for you. You always help others. I know I can trust you.

You: It's OK. But I have already planned to do some other tasks. I think it would not be appropriate to alter their schedules.

SP: You are talking weird things. Whatever you think may not be appropriate. This task is really important.

You: I can't say. I am not sure.

SP: Leave it now. We can argue throughout the day. Time is fleeting. You wouldn't disappoint me. Would you?

You: I feel that.....

SP: Alright! I know I can count on you. Here is the address. See you again.

Do you see your own image in this example? Do you use the same language (of this example) when you talk to others? This example tells us that you cannot say 'no' directly and that you use an uncertain language even as you surrender before the other person. The other person knows very well how your hesitation and decency can be used against you.

In other words, you allow yourself to be used. The tasks that you do not want to do are done by you. If you continue to work according to the will of others and be reluctant to say 'no', the anger and dissent within you would continue to swell. That way, you would harm yourself. When this anger and feeling of suffocation reaches a peak, an explosive situation would be created. At times, the anger would come out and hit the right target but in most cases, it would be expressed in a wrong way.

In order to escape this situation, read another example.

SP: Would you do a task for me?

You: But tell me first what the task is?

SP: A packet has come for me from the transport office. You go by car and fetch that packet.

You: But I don't think I would be able to fetch it. I would have to remain busy throughout the day.

SP: How does it matter if you go for a while? See, I would remain trapped here for the day. Someone has to bring it.

You: Why should I do the tasks of taking things to places or bringing them to you? I am fed up by your demands. Why don't you think about doing your own tasks?

SP: What has happened to you? I had given you a simple task.

You: Nothing has happened to me all of a sudden. You never give ordinary tasks to me. You do not think about the convenience or discomfort of others. You think only about yourself. Why don't you fetch the packet yourself?

SP: Be calm. OK! OK! I won't give you any task in the future.

You: That would be appropriate.

Do you recognize this dialogue?

Is it familiar? You show dissent in it. But do you get

any benefit? In this conversation, you accuse the other person. The speed of conflict increases all of a sudden.

Or, it is also possible that you continue to increase the dispute and the real issue may be lost somewhere. Now, read the following example.

SP: Would you do one task for me?

You: First of all, tell me—what's the task?

SP: A packet has come from outside. It is lying at Transport Nagar. You go by car and bring it to me.

You: But I don't think I would be able to bring it. I would have to remain busy throughout the day.

SP: How does that matter if you go for a while? Someone has to bring it. See, I shall be trapped here throughout the day.

You: You always give me one task or the other, whereas you know how much busy I am.

SP: How can I learn that you remain so busy? If you do not want to do my task, refuse in a clear manner.

You: I have not said that I cannot do it. I want you to think about it.

SP: What do you want to say? I am unable to understand.

You: What you cannot understand? I was saying.

SP: I know what you were saying. You were stating that I am harsh and never take care of you.

You: I never said so. Whatever I said is being wrongly understood by you. You always do so—you listen to only that talk which you want to listen to.

SP: Now, why are you accusing me?

You: I am not accusing you. Do not create a mountain of a mole hill.

SP: So, you want to say that I create a mountain of a mole hill.

This argument continues. The talk of bringing the packet from the transport office is lost midway.

During this discussion, both sides try to look down upon each other. They try to prove that they are right. Thus, the real issue is forgotten. Do you think that this episode is somewhat familiar to you?

In the first conversation, you were reluctant and could never say clearly. What you wanted. In the second conversation, you became ready for direct conflict, whereas you know that if you got into conflict, you may have to withdraw and say sorry. In the third conversation, you try to while away the time by doing useless talk but are not able to reach a result.

In the end of each of these conversations, you find yourself in an uncomfortable situation, for arguments are not liked and there is no result either. Hence, it is decided that you would mind it and your opinion would be strengthened—how much capable you are in resolving a conflict. And this is true that noble people are incapable of resolving conflict. There are three main reasons due to which people feel that they are incapable of handling conflict.

The first reason is that in the beginning of conflict, you form an opinion that you would lose. Most noble people find themselves in a weak position at the time of conflict. They think, "Whatever may be the issue, I shall give up." So, your psyche has already decided to accept defeat and there is a feeling to flee even before the conflict starts. When you assume that you would lose, you are likely to lose in most cases.

The second reason is—fear of outcome. When you start conflict, you have to put your foot forward in an unknown battlefield. You do not know what's going to happen. This can be known only when you handle the conflict with determination. You can make a person angry. Someone can cry or throw something at you. Or, he can mishandle you in physical terms. Since you do not know, you try your best to avoid conflict.

The reason is – the memories of the moments of conflict in your family can motivate you to keep clear of any conflict. If your parents fought when you were a child and you did not like it, or you used to feel helpless (as a child) to stop your parents from fighting, this kind of helplessness, this feeling, can dominate you even after you become an adult. Thus, at the time of conflict, you may feel at your wit's end. You may become so much obsessed with the old emotional experiences of your childhood that it may become difficult for you to differentiate between the emotional experiences of past and present.

There can be other reasons behind the phenomenon of avoiding conflict. It is important for you to identify them. But basically, there are three such reasons as keep you away from conflict. Before knowing that, let us know why conflict takes place.

Why Does This Happen?

Why does conflict take place? There has to be a reason behind it. The chief reasons are as follows:

- The will to win.
- Making the other person aware of your opinion.
- Getting your work done.
- To let people know that they are in the wrong.
- Deciding your own limits.
- Establishing your own supremacy.
- Stopping your misuse or exploitation.

There are many such reasons which we consider to be the background of conflict, although none of them is the real reason. The conflict may be of commercial type or totally personal, there is only one reason behind it. The reason is – the objective of conflict is to reach a conclusion.

Be that a commercial or personal type of conflict, most people do not choose struggle to find out a solution. They do so in most cases because they think that they are right. And when they think that they are right, someone else has to be in the wrong.

That dispute can be anything. You can say that the other person's land is yours. You can say that you are superior to God, or you want to establish your supremacy over others. Most types of conflict are concerned with victory or loss when you try to impose your will on others.

When you would like to face conflict with the reasons mentioned above, no solution would come up. If you do away with your will and accept the will of the other party, the conflict comes to an end. If you get excited, and then, you say sorry and add that you were in the wrong, the conflict comes to an end. If you remain stubborn and state that your action was logical, the conflict does not come to an end. The issue may be subdued for some time but it can crop up before you at a later date.

None of these situations has any solution.

The attitude of the countries in conflict with other countries indicates clearly that they are not keen to have solutions. They are keen only to win.

Similarly, the decades-old court case between two families can be viewed in the same perspective. New generations also continue the case, for they are not interested in a solution. They want to prove that they are right. So, no one pays attention to the basic reason behind the dispute.

Some husband-wife pious can be seen in society who start fighting over trifles. They repeat the old sets of logic and argument for years. They are not keen to find out solutions. They fight with freedom, for they feel that their freedom has come in danger due to their marriage.

When your self-pride is hurt, your emotional experiences are hurt. Your dignity is hurt. Your sensitivity is attacked. Questions are raised about your perseverance. Your ability is put under the cloud of suspicion. Your dedication is censured. Then, you get peeved or angry and want to attack.

If you do not get ready to face conflict, you would never get solutions. Your emotional experiences would be suppressed and unpleasant conditions would not change either. If you are excessively noble, you would not oppose even after getting hurt and would continue to act, as if nothing has happened. Thus, the heap of injuries, attacks (on you), criticism, and other feelings would keep on accumulating inside you.

Whenever you stand in front of a conflict, you have also the history of getting defeated and giving up with you. This means that you try to put across your point on one issue. Then, many unresolved issues also struggle to come up.

So, can the noble people get any solution at any point of time?

Solution of Conflict

In order to solve a problem, we have to find its solution. Doing so is a good thing. If the objective of struggle is to reach a solution, why don't I find a solution through my own way? Why don't I tell the other person that his solution is wrong? Why don't I tell him that my solution is correct? Why getting sorry from someone is not a solution?

All these can seem to be the forms of solution but when you hurt a person in the same manner in which you were hurt, it means that you have not solved the problem. You are thinking about victory eve now. Telling the other person about your grievance can be part of solution but if that is your real objective, you cannot go much further.

In order to resolve conflict or satisfy both (warring) factions, you must take care of the following aspects:

- Do not play blame games.
- Continue or extend the discussion.
- Find out why you do not have the things that you want.
- Change yourself to change others.

Before discussing these aspects, it is important to ponder over the issue that correct and objective-oriented thoughts are needed to put an end to conflict. Whatever behaviour you show towards the conflict, is your habit. It is like all other good habits that you have. Hence, you have to become alert towards changing your method of dealing with conflict.

Do Not Accuse

When you are unhappy, you use accuse others, that is your first attack weapon for defending your own self. "It's his fault." "He has done this." When something does not happen according to our will, we accuse others on account of failure. If you have been collecting heaps of dejection, lassitude and anger throughout your life, this happens quite often. In such a situation, you consider it appropriate to put the entire blame on the person with who you are in conflict, even if the person concerned may have nothing to do with your lassitude.

Most of such sentences start with 'you'. "You think only about your own self." "You always expect me to do what you wish for." In such sentences, the words like 'never' and 'always' are also included. You become emotional and keep on flowing. Thus, you deviate from the main issue.

If you do not want to accuse, you would have to become

aware of your emotional experiences and understand what impact the situation has on you. Further, you would have to start your statement with 'I', not 'you.'

In the context of struggle, if you begin your statement with 'you,' it means that the other person is being held accountable for the problem at hand. He is being thrown in a corner. He is being taken to be in the wrong. He is being incited to adopt a defensive posture.

Let us study an example.

"You never think about me."

"I always take care of you."

"When?"

"Many times."

A statement started with 'you' indicates the weakness of the person who is being addressed. No one wants to be proved wrong.

Think about yourself for a moment. Can you recall a dispute in which you had started your statement with 'you'? It happens in such conditions – we deviate from the main issue and start making efforts to save our own selves.

The subject is separated from the problem. Two parties accuse each other at the personal level. A woman wants her husband to help her in household chores and tells him, "You never help me in household tasks." Her husband starts the dispute and says, "I do my share of the task." The wife says, "No, you don't." The husband repeats, "I do."

If you say, "You do things according to your own will. You take decisions without asking me," such a statement would accuse the other person of something. So, he would adopt a defensive posture. Instead, you can state, "If you are supposed to take the decision next time, I would like to discuss it with you in advance."

In this statement, the element of control is visible. You are not responsible towards your own emotional experiences alone. Rather, you are telling the other person in certain terms what you want. The more responsible you become towards your own emotional experiences and desires, the less would be the need, in your mind, to highlight the limitations of the other person.

Here, a note should be read with vigil. There are many people who do not want to dump the idea of achieving victory or proving others wrong. They also use 'I.' "I feel that you cannot do if. I feel that you are careless."

The use of 'I' is less lethal while telling the other person how his behaviour or talk is making an impact on you. "You never ask what I want to do." We should not say this. We should say, "When you tell me to do a task that I do not want to do, I feel neglected. I cannot say no to you."

The first statement is not clear. There is a tinge of accusation in it. The second statement is clear. In it, you tell about emotional experiences and the other person does not have to adopt a defensive posture.

Extending the Discussion in a Forward Direction

This notion is important for those people who deviate from the main topic during the course of discussion and beat about the bush. Both parties feel dejected. Old wounds and failures start coming in front of us in the new reality.

Such types of dispute can be seen in most cases. Upon seeing them, one can understand why a thought must be present to resolve a conflict. Once you start taking rounds, it becomes difficult to stop the speed. The culmination of this is in the form of tears, banging the door or breaking an article.

Becoming dejected would not be solution. Different attitude is needed to continue a dialogue further. If some gap is put in discussion, both parties can think about the direction of discussion, and they can turn it towards a more creative direction.

Let us study the following example.

You: What you want to say? I had said only this.

Second Person (SP): I know what you had said. You had said that I am cruel and never think about you.

You: I think that we should stop here. That's because I feel that we are repeating a single thing. I feel that we are trying to look down upon each other and so moving away from the main issue. We must start afresh and try to understand the problem properly.

You kill two birds with one stone if you follow this tactic. You stop endless arguments. Besides, you stop the game of allegation and counter-allegation and decide the joint responsibility for the next round of discussion.

Making the Bridge

This means – giving the other person something so that he may be keen or willing to give something in lieu of it. When you are expecting emotional excitement in lieu of conflict, giving anything to the other person can prove to be objectionable to you. "Why should I give him, given that his behavior towards me is so rough?"

Giving something to the other person does not mean that you accept his supremacy. We can see the example, given earlier, in this perspective.

Second Person (SP): Would you do a task for me?

You: What is it?

SP: A packet has come from outside. It is lying at the Transport Nagar. You go by car and get it.

You: You are telling me to do this task at a wrong hour. I am sorry. I won't be able to do it.

SP: But I am sure. Only you can do it.

You: I am glad to learn that you trust me so much. You must be having many tasks at hand at this point of time.

SP: Really, there are many. I am unable to understand from which one I should start. All are equally important. So, I need your help.

You: I can see what type of stress you are under. But I am really sorry to tell you that I won't be able to go to the transport office. It won't be possible for me to go out. But why should we ponder over the tasks that you have at hand? Let's take ten minutes to do so. Let us clear some files. Then, we shall see if someone else can go to the transport office. We can persuade another person to do so.

You do not know, in certain terms, whether the desired outcome would come up or not. But you have changed the direction of discussion and given him the reference of a third person. So, you have given the direction of another person who may do the task. Besides, you have proposed how you can help him. This help can be of great use to him. In the meantime, you can also think about the problem of bringing the packet.

The word 'no' has not been used even once here.

But the way this conflict was resolved, it has been ensured that a limit can be defined and a clear stand can be adopted to say 'no' to anyone. This is an art in itself.

Think about making the bridge and keep many alternatives as building blocks so that the other person may be able to choose one alternative from among those (given by you). You expressed your sympathy towards the other person in this case. After this, you presented your viewpoint in a lucid manner and stated that you won't be able to do the task. There was no alibi or subtle talk. There was no accusation either. And in the end, you offered some sort of help. It was not big help but you showed the desire to become a helper in the process of reducing the present problem.

This means that you put three bricks (from your side) to build the bridge. The other person has some new alternatives. It is also possible that the other person may refuse to accept your bricks. He may continue o make efforts to get his proposal accepted, or he may continue the argument. Or, he may think that it he gets your help for ten minutes, he can be benefited. Thus he can complete his tasks in an organized manner and think about getting the packet.

The process of building bridge can prove to be an effective method to connect a new dimension in respect of disagreement. Through this, you can become or remain helpful and sympathetic towards the other person with bending down. Through it, the useless arguments can also be done away with.

Finding Out Why You Do Not Get What You Want

Sometimes, there is no solution available for the fulfillment of your specific desire. Sometimes, it does not happen due to the circumstances you are in. And you are forced to accept those circumstances. Then, we agree that during the course of present set of circumstances, there was no other solution for gaining victory.

Why don't you get what you want? If we find out the reason, our lassitude can come down. But whatever you want, you do not get. If you want to find out why that is so, you do not have the right to put the other person in a circle of questions. If you do so, your nature of accusing others may be highlighted.

After doing general analysis, you can get an opportunity to tell the other person about your emotional experiences. When you find out what you want but do not get, you do not feel that you are very angry with the person who does not want to give you the thing desired by you. That's because you are highly enlightened. Let's then towards the conversation that was discussed in the beginning.

Second Person (SP): Would you do my task?

You: Let's know what is it?

SP: A packet has come from outside. It is lying at the Transport Nagar. You go by car and bring that packet.

You: It would not be convenient for me to go there today. It would be difficult for me to do this task.

SP: But I trust you. Only you can do this task.

You: In such conditions, I feel, I am being misused. Can't you tell any other person to bring that packet? If I do not drive the car outside the city, I would feel relieved.

SP: I am not misusing you. I am really trapped. I had forgotten about the packet. Now, I do not have any other option but to tell you to drive the car up to the transport office. I would remember your help and reciprocate for this favour of yours.

You: OK! I shall bring. But I need the remuneration.

SP: What remuneration?

You: You would thank me ten times, and do three tasks for me in the future.

Changing Yourself to Change Others

The discussion done so far clearly tells us that you have to intervene to change the course of conversation. You have to avoid the game of accusation. You have stop useless discussion and change the direction of conflict. You have to present alternatives. You have to find out the reasons and analyze the same.

In order to do something different, you have to change the old trend. In other words, if you want to change yourself, you would have to change your own self first. For excessively noble people, this is very difficult. They feel that other people may change first so that they may not have to interfere.

Those people, who want others to change, use these words, "If he..." or "There is no person who has not said anything like this in one second of his life." Or "Had he got the job, I would have become safe" or, "If she shuts up, I would be able to leave a sign of relief." Or "If he stops praising himself, talks can be started." Or, "If he tells how he is feeling, I would understand that I am not being ignored."

Hence, you want other persons to change so that you may feel better. In such a condition, your role is similar to that of a passive and tortured person. Such a person waits for others to change to get things in his own favour. You put the responsibility on other people for whatever is happening and thus expect to change the outcomes of the situation in question.

It also means that you are unable to control your life. You wait for your life to have change and expert that if other persons would wish, everything would be according to your desire. If you are waiting for the other person to change to put your own house in order, your wait would never end.

If you want to influence the result of planned behaviour between other persons and your own self, you would have to play an active role. You would have to accept the accountability of your emotional experiences and desires and take steps after careful thinking to obtain different results.

●

18

Change Your Behaviour to Learn the Art of Saying 'No'

When you behave in a noble way for a long period, people do not think it necessary to ponder over your complaints later. They do not listen to you, especially the talk that they don't want to listen to. They do not care for such kind of talk. They get accustomed to approvals from your end and so, they do not expect any kind of refusal from your side. This means that if you try to put across your viewpoint, or if you put up a demand, you would be ignored.

If want to become an expert in the art of saying 'no,' you would have to learn the process of attracting the attention of others. Here, some similar methods have been discussed that can be followed with case.

Mutual Consent

It is an important method. It can be used easily. It affects the situation in a most effective manner and quickly. You can take the role of controller, to change the direction of conversation, by using it. If someone is attacking you, you can try this technique and throw him off the track.

What would you do when a person is trying to dominate you and not stopping? At that time, you would like to soothe him and calm down his excitement and remind him of the fact that he is crossing his limits.

Try to agree with him. If he tells you that you are useless, agree with him. Then say, "You are probably correct. I am useless." If someone says, "You have wasted your life," tell him, "You are correct. I have wasted my life." If someone says, "You don't know what you are doing," tell him, "You are right. I am unable to understand what I am doing." Here, the objective is to stop the attacks of the other person and disarm him.

A normal defensive conversation goes on like this.

Second Person (SP): You are useless.

You: No, this is not the case.

SP: I have told you—you are useless. You cannot do a single task properly. I had told you to do one small task and you have spoiled it.

You: No, it is not spoiled. I am sure we shall achieve our goal.

SP: Yes, but I myself would have to make effort to do so.

When you agree with the other person, the conversation would be as follows.

SP: You are a useless fellow.

You: You are right. I am useless.

SP: That's what I want to say. See this spoiled task.

You: Really? What has gone wrong with it? You must not trust me for a single minute. You must be having a way to rectify it.

SP: Why did you do so?

You: I don't know. I made a mistake. What do you think?

There is a magical effect on the attacking person. This kind of agreement is a better tool for those people who are excessively noble, for they do not have to criticize the other person while using it.

When you express your consent, the other person

adopts a defensive posture. Every time, the other person criticizes you. And every time, you show that you agree with him. Thus, it becomes difficult for the other person to take the next step. It's just possible that he may say to you, "Alright! But you need to improve." Again, your reply should show agreement. You should say, "You are absolutely right. I need to rectify myself." Such a type of agreement proves to be effective.

Take Time

Those people, who are excessively noble, give immediate reply to the demands of the other persons. Someone rings you up and asks for an answer to resolve a problem. Someone else would impose his will on you and force you to say 'yes.' Someone would invite you to participate in a programme or attend a party and he would expect an immediate reply from your end. He would expect you to say, "I shall certainly come. I would be pleased to attend."

In all these cases, other persons want that answer from you which they expect. You generally give them a reply as well. Although you want to say 'no,' your emotional experiences dominate you to such an extent that you say 'yes.' You give an answer that, you think, others would like to hear. That way, you do not take care of your own interests. So, you start getting regulated according to the commands of the other person. You dump your own wish. It seems that other people have started controlling your life, even if it is very inconvenient for you to work according to the will of others.

The difficult here is that you start working according to the will of others and do not pay attention to your own will. So, you do not know that you like to attend a party or programme, or you are forced to marry someone (against your wish). Emotional experiences dominate your personality and you stop thinking about your own self.

When you take some time to think, you would be able to escape the flow of the emotional experiences. That way, you would be able to take correct decisions. You would be able to decide your next step by assessing the situation in a correct manner. There are many ways for taking time. You can use many alibis to do so. Some examples follow:

- You have told me to do this task at the wrong time. I shall contact you later.
- I have to go to toilet. I shall come back and talk to you.
- I think there is someone at the door. I shall ring you up after some time.
- I can think about it properly only after taking a cup of coffee. Then, I shall ring you up and tell you.

You can use an alibi of any type. Use such an alibi as should not demand an answer from your at that instant only. By using that alibi, you would be separated from that situation and then, you would be able to decide what is right or wrong.

Take time to think and think deeply. Separate yourself from the situation in such a manner that the control of the other person over you is totally removed. Whatever you want to do, please go ahead and do that task. Walk around in the room. Take deep breaths. Do something so that your attention may shift away from other person's control.

You would not do so because you have to say 'no.' It is just possible that you may not know till now that you have to say 'no.' It is possible that you may not even know till now that you have to say 'no.' You may not know that you have to say 'Yes.' It's just possible that the demand of the other person may be justified and you may like to state 'yes.' But the brain must be stable to take an exact decision. Instead of agreeing according to the will of others, you must take a decision on the basis of your perseverance.

It's possible that you may give an answer after thinking and understanding (the problem at hand) that you could have given in a Jiffy. But the difference is that your answer would not be given without thinking carefully and it would not be a decision taken under pressure of other people. You select your choice like you never used to do before.

When you take time, you ponder over the issue slowly. You look at all the aspects of the problem. Then, the decision you take is not the one taken in a Jiffy. Taking time means heading towards victory. It does not mean the ability to say 'no.'

Cut Down Your Speed

One can reduce one's speed by not dissociating completely from a situation. You can say, "Can't you explain slowly? At this speed, it is difficult for me to understand." Or, you can say, "If you repeat what you have said, I would be able to comprehend in a much better manner." By using statements like these, the speed of discussion can be reduced and that way, you can get more time to think.

If you are one among those people who do not like to express their hesitation, you would agree for that talk also which you have not understand.

Most people do not like silence. It seems to be very inconvenient to them. Most people say something to break silence during the course of a conversation to escape the feeling of inconvenience.

You can play a kind of game here. It is a game that involves keeping quiet. Most people must have tried it at one point or the other in their life. It is a competition for remaining silent. It means, "I shall keep quiet till the time you speak." When you remain silent, you may feel uneasy but since you are doing this deliberately, the other person may feel troubled because of your silence.

If you practice this game, you would be able to use it in a best manner while taking a decision. Silence is an effective weapon which can be used to cut the noose being tightened around your neck by the other person.

If it is not possible to completely remain silent according to the situation you are in, you can create small intervals (of silence). During the course of discussion, you can give brief answers and thus create intervals. Give your view point in a clear yet brief manner and then, keep quiet.

Say 'No' with Alacrity

A perfect method of saying 'no' is—say 'no' with alacrity. Whenever a demand is made—any type of demand—say 'no' at the maximum possible speed and at your earliest. Then, you can give a reason or ask for forgiveness. You can tell him all the reasons in a noble manner. You may say, "I am really sorry. I know you would mind it, for I have said 'no.'" You can continue, "I hope you would forgive me." And so on. If you are afraid of saying 'no' directly, mix this 'no' in your conversion. It must be wrapped up in a decent, nice language so that your 'no' may not have any adverse effect.

Read the following example:

A: I want you to sit here late in the right and prepare this report:

B: No! I won't be able to do it tonight. I am sorry. I really want to help you but it is impossible tonight. I am really very sorry.

Wait for a Minute

It is a brief and easy statement. We can use it to take time. As soon as you feel that you mouth is going to utter 'yes' (even if you want to say 'no'), say immediately, "Wait for one minute." Or, if you feel that someone is changing the direction of discussion which is opposite to the one you have decided, tell him, "Please wait for one minute."

Some examples are as follows:

- "Wait for one minute, did I want to say this only?"
- "Wait for one minute; I am not sure what I think about it."
- "Wait for a minute; I want to say something more."
- "Wait for a minute; it would be appropriate to learn what we people think about it."

That way, you stop the flow of conversation and are able o control your own self. Then, we can analyze and scan our thoughts and that way, we earn a small victory.

Changing Thoughts

This stage is the one that comes after "Please wait for a minute." In other words, you withdraw after a circumstance passes. When you feel that you have made a mistake (after one hour, two days or three weeks), what do you think them? What would you like to do then?

You can feel that you have to go according to the will of the other person. You can feel that you do not have the right to change your thought. "I have given my word. Now, I cannot refuse." You think that once you give your word, you cannot go back on your word; it is impossible to do so. Why can't you deny (what you had promised earlier)?

After a circumstance passes, you feel that you cannot do anything to change it. Whatever has been said is an inscription on stone. You have said 'yes' for something and now, you cannot go back from your word. This is not correct.

Other people generally change their thoughts. You become a victim of such types of change. There may be countless people who would have broken their promises made to you and said to themselves, "I shall always be true to my words." This is a good spirit. But due to this type of thinking, you can be in trouble.

You have the right to change your thoughts. You may do so after five minutes or one month. You can say, while changing your thought, "I made a mistake. I am sorry. You would face trouble but I cannot do it."

●